DESERT

D0260231

Bodie is trailing a trio of escapees from Yuma Pen — three men he'd helped to put there in the first place. But when they shoot his horse out from under him, he finds himself adrift in the searing desert. If he's to turn the tables on those now hunting him, he needs to reach the life-saving waters at Pinto Wells. But there's another shock awaiting him. A face from his past. A man supposed to be dead. A killer who's tracked Bodie down, and plans to exact his own vengeance . . .

NEIL HUNTER

DESERT RUN

Complete and Unabridged

LINFORD
Leicester

First published in Great Britain in 2015

First Linford Edition
published 2016

A catalogue record for this book is available
from the British Library.

ISBN 978–1–4448–3006–4

Published by
F. A. Thorpe (Publishing)
Anstey, Leicestershire

Set by Words & Graphics Ltd.
Anstey, Leicestershire
Printed and bound in Great Britain by
T. J. International Ltd., Padstow, Cornwall

This book is printed on acid-free paper

Prologue

His Apache name at birth had been Massai yet when he had grown and become a hunter of men he became known as Silverbuck . . .

The Spanish word for him was *Mestizo*. To the *Pinda Lickoyi* he was a half-breed. His father had been a full-blood Mescalero warrior, his mother a young Mexican captive. His mother had died when he was ten years old and he had been raised within the family of his father, though never fully accepted by the tribe. When he was seventeen years old, already a proven fighter, Massai's father was killed, along with a few other Apaches in a fight with the American cavalry in the rocky escarpments of the Canyon de Chelly.

His mother had taught him Spanish and a cousin of his father coached him in English. By the time he reached his grown age he was conversant in both languages as well as his native tongue.

With the deaths of his parents behind him and feeling unsettled due to his divergent bloodline he saw the isolation developing. It drove him away from the tribe and he took to living in two worlds. With his language skills he was able to pass among the Mexicans and Americans, dressing their way and remaining observant and at the same time quiet and subservient. His existence on the fringes of society allowed him to pass unnoticed and he learned to listen and not talk, picking up information that would be of use to him. At first he took on small jobs that enabled him to employ his Apache skills, though he played on his Mexican heritage which allowed him to move with less challenges. He tracked wanted men from the posters displayed and found he was good at this.

Slowly his reputation built as he succeeded with each new hunt. From the start he asked to be paid in silver dollars. It became his trademark and before long he was being addressed by this affectation. By then he had become addicted to the lure of ready money his skills with the gun could bring and with each success his reputation grew. In addition to his man hunting he began to hire out his gun, unmindful of the reasons *why* he was being employed.

So the half-breed Massai became the man hunter and gunman known as Silverbuck. He had chosen his path and found there was ample work for someone with his talents.

He favored the impassive face of his people, his dark skin held tight over pronounced cheekbones, though the left one showed where it had once been broken. His black hair was chopped back to his neck, because it made him look more Mexican than Apache and helped him move around in the white man's world, though he favored a traditional Apache headband that kept his hair away from his face. When he was on the hunt he abandoned his white man's clothing and wore a faded blue shirt, a pair of washed-out Levis and *N'deh b'keh*, the traditional, high Apache footwear. Around his waist hung a simple leather belt that supported the leather holster and the much-used .45 caliber Colt's Peacemaker. A broad-bladed knife was sheathed on his left side. He also favored a .44-40 Winchester rifle with a cut-down barrel and stock. It went everywhere with him and was at his side when he slept. In a thick hide pouch, slung around his waist, Silverbuck carried additional loads for both rifle and pistol. He was proficient with them all and had no hesitation using them when needed.

This day he squatted on a rocky outcrop, indifferent to the blistering heat, his gaze fixed on the lone figure moving slowly across the desert flats. A tall *Pinda Lickoyi*, he was known to Silverbuck. Alone and on foot, his steps slow and uncertain as he crossed the forbidding emptiness of the wasteland, he no longer appeared a threat to the lone Apache warrior as he had on other occasions.

The big man was what the *Pinda Lickoyi* called a bounty hunter. He hunted men down for the rewards posted on them as did Silverbuck. Silverbuck knew this man as a powerful warrior. Swift with the gun he carried and merciless when he tracked his quarry.

Among the *Pinda Lickoyi* he was known as The Stalker.

Silverbuck knew him by his given name . . . he was called Bodie.

And he was the man Silverbuck had come to kill.

They had clashed when Silverbuck had taken a contract to side with men who were hired to seek Bodie. In a violent confrontation between them, the breed had barely survived. He had been left for dead by the man hunter. His face badly marked from Bodie's attack, an arm and ribs broken and his throat slit open by a savage knife cut. If Bodie had not been in a running fight with others he might have seen Silverbuck still lived. Barely able to move, having lost much blood, the Apache had dragged himself away, found his horse and had ridden quietly from the scene after tightly binding his neck with strips of cloth cut from a shirt. He had travelled far enough to take him away from Bodie and had ridden out of the *brasada*. Back to the land of the Apache.

More dead than alive Silverbuck had reached the place of an old Apache who practiced the healing arts. The Apache's primitive home had been isolated in the unbleached high country, far from prying eyes. The old man saw to Silverbuck's injuries, setting the broken arm, binding his ribs and sewing the gash in his throat. The treatment was basic but it closed the wound, leaving a thick, ragged scar. What the Mexican could not do was repair the internal damage to Silverbuck's vocal cords and when his wound healed the breed found he was left with virtually no ability to speak. Anything he said came out as a low, harsh whisper of sound. Silverbuck stayed with the Apache for over three months, letting his ravaged body heal as best it could. He had lost two teeth and his nose, broken in the fight, though reset by the old man, had remained off center. The broken cheekbone showed as a lump beneath the skin. None of these things worried Silverbuck. He had no vanity where his looks were concerned. He was a warrior, not a weak woman concerned over her appearance.

Over the long weeks of his slow recovery Silverbuck was barely able to eat while his mouth healed and he was in considerable pain. He accepted his limitations because he was Apache in spirit and the Apache bore pain and suffering as part of life. The old man brought Silverbuck Apache remedies that offered relief from the pain. There were herbs and plants that offered pain relief, known only to the healers for generations. And the Apache gave Silverbuck *Peyote* to calm his spirits and allow him the visions so he could pass the long days and nights in a restive stupor.

While he rested, slowly gaining in strength, Silverbuck saw in his mind what he needed to do in order to restore his spirit. He understood the need for vengeance. It was a feeling he had carried inside himself for a long time.

And when he was recovered and able to move on he left the old Apache's place and took to the even higher ground to brood and make his plans.

He understood he was now more alone than he had ever been. Many of *The People* were ready to surrender to the whites. Their days were numbered if they remained at war. It had become a lost cause and though many Apaches understood the changes might not be the best way it had become a choice between life or death. The leaders looked at the starving, sick children. Saw the inevitable end of the Apache way and they counseled their people to lay down their weapons and submit to the law of the whites. The majority did this but there were a few who stood apart and refused, determined to fight on.

Silverbuck was one of those. He took himself into the mountain fastness, up high where few could follow, using the age-old Apache trails that remained unknown to the *Pinda Lickoyi*. Here, in the sun-baked emptiness Silverbuck made his camps, moving often, only emerging when he needed to replenish his food supplies and to make raids on isolated homesteads where he gained more plunder. Building his store of ammunition. Taking anything that appealed to him. And always driven by his desire to find the man called Bodie so he could claim his revenge.

He found his lone status worked for him and it also allowed him the freedom to search for the man called Bodie. Over long months Silverbuck searched. Sought information about the man. It was difficult keeping track. As a man hunter Bodie travelled far and wide, often going great distances that took him away from the haunts of the Apache.

One of the Apache's few contacts, always willing to trade information for the white man's whisky, or money, spent much time around one of the Army posts and it was from this man Silverbuck received news that Bodie was back in the southwest area on the hunt for *Pinda Lickoyi* who had escaped the prison on the Colorado. From his man Silverbuck heard that it had been Bodie who captured the men and had them imprisoned in the place called Yuma. Silverbuck knew about the prison. It was a bad place where men existed in a living hell. That these men had escaped might not have interested Silverbuck but when he learned Bodie had been asked to go after them he became very interested.

Bodie's pursuit of the escapees brought him into Silverbuck's territory. His hunting ground. It was a chance he could not ignore. An opportunity to claim his vengeance on the man hunter. To make him suffer long before he died.

Knowing this allowed Silverbuck to become a watcher over the chase. It pleased him to watch it unfolding. As much as Silverbuck wanted to see Bodie die, he was also ready to witness the outcome as the chase took place.

So he stayed out of sight and would remain that way until the pursuit below reached its climax and it was his turn to take on Bodie.

Silverbuck could have killed Bodie even now, from where he sat. Yet he held back because there was reason to stay his hand. The Apache was waiting to see the outcome of the events that had brought Bodie to this place. He was curious. And he wanted to see how the game played itself out.

One of the three whites had shot

Bodie's horse from under him. The man hunter had evaded them but they had pushed him into the desert and now they were forcing him to run ahead of them.

Silverbuck saw the three whites had a strong hate for Bodie. He understood their feelings. Bodie had been instrumental in having them convicted and sent to Yuma where they had spent three long years in the brutal prison. It would have been with them the whole time. And when they escaped, as Silverbuck carried his need for vengeance, they would want the chance to get even with the man who had taken away those years.

As he sat and watched the scene below Silverbuck rubbed a calloused hand back and forth across the ridged scar on his neck. It remained as a permanent reminder of what Bodie had done to him. More than the scars around his mouth, or the cheekbone that had remained distorted, even the ache in his arm that came and went.

The knife wound to his throat, leaving him with barely the ability to speak, had affected him more than any other wound.

Bodie had left him for dead but Silverbuck had survived and he would follow the *Pinda Lickoyi* until the time came for him to strike . . .

1

One minute he had been following the trail leading across the sun-blasted Arizona desert, his concentration on the faint hoof prints, when the sound of a rifle broke the silence. Bodie felt the horse beneath him shudder. It gave a harsh cough, snorting blood, and then went down, taking him with it. He had the presence of mind to clear the stirrups before the bulk of the dun-colored horse collapsed. Bodie swung sideways, wanting to clear the heavy bulk to avoid getting trapped. He hit the dry dust of the ground, taking the weight on his left shoulder, the impact sending a burst of pain through him. He rolled, half reaching his feet, then went down again and caught a mouthful of the fine alkaline dust. The sudden hard landing kicked the breath from his lungs and he was immobile for long seconds. Seconds he hated to lose because close, or near, there was someone out there with a long gun and they were always that much more accurate than any revolver. The second he was able to draw a solid breath again he got his hands under him and pushed upright, turning fast and diving over the bulk of the downed horse, pulling himself into cover. The rifle shot had come from his right, so his move put the horse between him and the unknown shooter.

He could taste the acrid alkaline dust in his mouth. Bodie spat but couldn't clear it all. He needed water to rinse it away and immediately remembered his canteen hanging from the saddle horn. Bodie slithered along the downed horse and raised himself in order to make a grab for the canteen. He hooked his fingers around the strap and pulled the canteen towards him.

The second shot smashed into the canteen, the lead slug going all the way through and burying itself in the saddle. Bodie felt water spurt from the bullet holes. He continued dragging the leaking canteen to him, ducking down again. Water was pulsing from the holes. He didn't spend time staring. Bodie took a swallow, rinsed his mouth and spat. With his mouth clear he was able to take a drink before the rest of the water drained away, letting the final dribbles run across his sweating face. He stared at the canteen for a moment before throwing it aside.

'Ain't lookin' too good for you, bounty man. No damn horse. Now no water. What you goin' to do?'

The shooter was taunting him. Knowing he had Bodie in a difficult position and was bound on letting him know.

'Now I see why Elkins didn't come back from pickin' up supplies. You done for him. Son of a bitch, now it's your turn.'

Bodie knew the owner of the voice. It wasn't one he was ever likely to forget.

16

Billy Dancer. Young. Mid-twenties. A whip-lean individual with a bad complexion, a livid scar down the right side of his face and receding pale hair, Billy Dancer was sick in the head. A scary individual with an overriding need to maim and destroy. Even at his comparatively young age Billy Dancer could lay claim to a number of kills. Dancer was known to be impulsive and took offence in a breath. As long as he had a gun in his hand Dancer believed himself immortal. Without a weapon he was nothing. Then he depended on his partners.

Tobe Benedict. Thick mustache drooping over his upper lip. Six foot tall, with a solid, powerful build. A man who was the complete opposite of Dancer, Benedict showed little in the way of fear, armed or not. He was a violent, brutal individual who held no one — or anything — in any kind of respect. Benedict saw the world as his for the taking and he lived by that code.

The third of the trio was the undoubted natural leader. The others all walked in his shadow. Followed his orders and never questioned him. His name was Vince Cagle. A sharp thinker when the need arose. A planner. And a man who would kill if his path was blocked.

In truth there *had* been five of them. Walt Elkins and a man named Teeler had made up the group. Like the rest Elkins had been a man who figured he had a right to take what was not his own.

2

Walt Elkins had masterminded the break. He had learned from one of the prison guards, during a long drinking session, that a work party would be assigned to repairing the public road a mile from the town of Yuma. There had been a partial collapse of a section of the road following a storm and the prison was going to supply a gang to be used on the reconstruction. Elkins had been trying to figure out how to work the escape for weeks. The work gang was like a wish come true. As soon as he found out he began to make his plans.

He kept his crew down to two men he knew he could trust and with two days to go before the prison crew was due to start Elkins made his preparations.

The work crew would be transported

from the prison by wagon. A big, heavy-wheeled wagon pulled by a pair of strong horses. There would be eight of them, accompanied by five armed guards from the prison. The crew would be hauled to the damaged section of the road, handed tools and put to work. It would be hard, digging and moving earth and rocks under the Arizona sun, but the men were long term prisoners, sent to Yuma to serve out their time in the harsh environment of the brutal regime. No one was going to show much sympathy for them and especially the time served guards who were not known for their soft attitude.

★   ★   ★

By eight o'clock the work crew was well into their long day. The only relief provided was a large wooden water butt strapped to the side of the wagon. There was a wooden ladle, fastened to the side of the butt, so the prisoners could help themselves to water. Under the blazing sun, breathing in dust and sweating heavily, the prisoners needed regular visits to refresh themselves. It was a known fact that most of the guards would have denied them the water if they had been given their way, but common sense dictated the need to replenish lost moisture or the prisoners would start dropping like flies.

By mid-morning the repair was progressing steadily. The work crew had developed a steady rhythm and the guards were starting to relax.

On one side of the road the ground sloped at an angle, stunted Palo Verde trees and mesquite dotting the slope. The vegetation was sparse, interspersed with a scattering of rocks. Not a great deal of cover but enough so that three men with rifles were able to converge and target the prison guards.

On a signal from Elkins the hidden shooters opened fire. The guards were caught unprepared and three of them went down in the first volley. Two died instantly. One man took two slugs through his back and dropped, rolling partway beneath the wagon. The horses, startled by the shooting, lunged forward, dragging the heavy wagon forward, one of the iron-rimmed wheels rolling over the wounded guard's head and crushing his skull.

The two guards still on their feet, responded to the ambush and returned fire at the concealed riflemen. They scored a hit on one of Elkin's men. The man went down with a rifle slug through his heart. Before either guard could find adequate cover behind the wagon, a concentrated volley from Elkins and his surviving man hit them both and they were dropped to the ground.

Elkins led the way down to the road where he greeted Cagle, Benedict and Dancer. He wasted no time.

'I got horses back there,' he said. 'Time we got away from here.'

Vince Cagle, as surprised as he might have been at the unexpected occurrence, recovered quickly.

'Damn right,' he said. 'Let's go, boys.'

Without a backward glance they followed Elkins, leaving the rest of the bewildered prisoners to their own devices. Within a mile they reached the spot where Elkins had horses and a change of clothes for them. The trio got rid of their striped prison garb and pulled on fresh clothing and boots. Elkins had handguns and rifles for them as well.

'Told you I wouldn't forget,' Elkins said.

'Took you three years to remember,' Billy Dancer grumbled.

'You always was an ungrateful son of a bitch,' Elkins said. 'This ain't been easy to fix. And I got a life to lead as well.'

'Don't pay him no mind,' Benedict said. 'Maybe we should have left him behind.'

They mounted up and rode away from the area, knowing that once the breakout was discovered the prison would be mounting a search. Indian trackers — Cocopah, Papago, Yaqui, were paid to hunt down anyone who escaped from the prison. Even Mexicans from across the border had been known to take up the chase. It didn't happen very often and any man who broke out would find himself being tracked by the Indians. The feeling was if a man was close to being caught by the trackers he might be better off dead. In this instance, with there being dead prison guards left behind, the hunt was going to be intense.

They rode clear of the area, Elkins knowing the territory better than most, and he was able to keep them ahead of anyone following.

'Those fellers back at Yuma are going to have their hands full with all the others who ran free,' Cagle said. 'That's got to help us.'

'We ain't clear yet,' Elkins pointed out.

'I'm not making light of it. Just suggesting with so many on the loose it takes some of the pressure off us.'

They made camp as soon as it got dark. Elkins had brought food that didn't need cooking and as much as they wanted a taste of hot coffee there was no way they were going to light a fire. Elkins had brought the next best thing. He broke out a couple of stone bottles of whisky.

'Man, that tastes good,' Benedict said as he took a swallow. 'Three years without is a cruel thing to make a man suffer.'

'Make it a perfect evening if you had a woman tucked away in those saddlebags,' Cagle said.

'Damn,' Elkins said, 'I knew I forgot something.'

'You going to be making jokes every damn day?' Dancer grumbled.

'If I've a mind to,' Elkins said. 'He never changes does he. Ungrateful bastard.'

'Pay him no mind,' Cagle said. 'Billy just doesn't see the funny side of anything.'

'Ain't much fun in being on the run,'

Dancer said peevishly.

'Maybe you'd prefer to be back in that hellhole,' Elkins said.

'Man has a point,' Benedict said.

Dancer went back to chewing on a piece of beef jerky.

'Time we talked business, Walt,' Cagle said. 'You know you'll get well paid for all this. I don't forget a friend.'

'Hell, Vince, I know that. But we have to play smart until it's safe to go for the cache. Wait until things quiet down. Law will be watching out for you going after that money. You never gave up the location all through your trial.'

'Three years down the line I ain't about to now. It's the only reason they didn't hang us. Kept us alive and locked up in Yuma figuring we might break and tell where it is.'

'Now you're out they'll be waiting on you going after it.'

'Mebbe so,' Benedict said, 'but they'll be sore disappointed when we don't.'

Elkins glanced across at him, worry etched across his face.

'Don't fret, Walt,' Cagle said. 'Tobe only means not for a while. Like you said, the law's going to be interested in where that cache is. So we let them stew on it. Take our time. It's not going anywhere . . . '

'And only Vince knows where it is,' Dancer said. 'So he needs to stay free and alive.'

'Safer that way,' Cagle said.

'Until you get you damned head blowed off.'

'Billy, have faith,' Elkins said.

'Faith ain't about to buy me what I want.'

'Same for all of us,' Benedict said.

'*Yeah*? You boys are gettin' older all the time. I'm still young. Got things to do an' places to go. I need my cut. Before I get *too* old to enjoy it.'

'Then you better make sure I don't step in the way of a bullet, boy.'

Elkin's partner, Teeler, a tall, skin and bone man had taken off to do some scouting for news. He was gone for the rest of the day and well into the next.

They moved to a new location before he got back, but Teeler knew where Elkins was going to be and found them camped out in a dry canyon where they had built their first cook fire beneath a wide overhang. It had been decided to take the risk because the high place they had chosen allowed them to see the surrounding country for a long way and there was no sign of any pursuit. When Teeler returned and tethered his horse the first thing he did was help himself to a tin mug of coffee.

Dancer, as usual, was the least patient, demanding to know what Teller had learned.

'Really wound up, aren't you boy,' Teeler said. 'You ever sit easy?'

Dancer would have stepped up to challenge him if Cagle had not pushed him back.

'Let the man take a breath, Billy. Happen he's had a long ride.'

'I rode through Yuma,' Teeler said. 'Some talk in town about what happened. Seems they got a search

28

goin' on around the border strip. They caught two of the fellers. One other tried to swim the river but drowned they say. I stayed with the crowd in one of the saloons and listened.'

'They still got the trackers out?' Benedict asked.

Teeler nodded. 'They's offerin' fifty dollars for every con the trackers bring in, and they ain't fussin' about dead or alive.'

'I figure I'm worth more than fifty dollars,' Dancer grumbled.

'Then you figured wrong,' Elkins said.

Teeler stepped close to Elkins and spoke to him quietly. Cagle noticed the move and caught Teeler's bony shoulder.

'*What?*' he asked.

Teeler glanced at him, then away.

'Walt? Damn it, no secrets here.'

Elkins rubbed at the back of his neck while he debated what to say. Then he realized there was no easy way to do it.

'The prison warden sent for Bodie.

He showed up while Teeler was in Yuma.'

'Big as life and lookin' like he had things to do,' Teeler said. 'Talk is the warden wanted him to track you three boys, seein' how he was . . . '

'Say it, Teeler,' Dancer snapped. ''Cause he was the one put us in the pen. For three damn years.' He spun round on Cagle. 'Money or not, we got a chance to put Bodie down for what he done. First we go after him, then collect our gold. Right, Vince? *Right?* It's what we talked about all the time we were locked away.'

Cagle didn't reply straight off. He stared across at Benedict. The man had a faint grin on his lips as he returned Cagle's glance.

'You up for this?' Cagle said.

'You really need to ask?' Benedict said.

Dancer gave a shrill laugh, gripping the Henry rifle he was holding. His lean face was flushed with excitement and he was already seeing Bodie dead and stretched out on the ground. He carried an obsessional desire to settled with the man hunter. He had talked about it incessantly during the long months in Yuma. It was more than simply personal for Billy Dancer. It drove him. Kept him going through the years behind Yuma's brutal walls, and while a driving force for the three of them, Dancer carried it further. There was no way he would walk away now Bodie was around. The feverish gleam in Dancer's eyes made Vince Cagle understand the younger man's desire for a showdown. And though he wanted a reckoning himself, Dancer's reaction to the news was unnerving . . . bringing back how it had happened three years ago . . .

3

. . . It all went well at first. They walked into the bank at Mesa mid-morning, dust drifting off their clothing as they trod the plank floor. The moment they stepped through the door they pulled up the scarves from around their necks and covered their faces before anyone could see them, easing the heavy .45 Peacemakers from their holsters and covering the bank staff and the single customer.

Billy Dancer, the youngest member of the gang, closed the door and stood guard, while Vince Cagle and Tobe Benedict bellied up to the counter, covering the three bank employees.

'Let's make this easy for everyone,' Cagle said. 'You all know why we're here. You have three satchels of gold coin in the vault. Came in last evening by Wells Fargo special delivery. I want

32

to see those satchels out front in the next couple of minutes. Mess me around and I will start by shooting the young woman in front of me. She'll be the first. Won't be the last.'

No one moved for a few seconds.

If the single customer had kept quiet he would have saved himself from injury. He didn't and it cost him after he rounded on Benedict who was standing close by.

'You believe we're going to take orders from you cowards? I won't allow you to threaten that young woman . . .'

Benedict turned with deliberate slowness as the man spoke. The way the corners of his eyes crinkled suggested he was smiling under his mask.

'Mistake,' he said. 'You should have kept your mouth closed.'

And then he used the solid weight of the revolver to slam again and again into the man's face. Even when the stunned figure fell back against the counter, blood pulsing from the ragged gashes in his face, his crushed nose and mouth, Benedict kept up the assault until the whimpering figure slid to the floor. His shirt and the jacket of his suit were wet with the blood coursing from his wounds.

Cagle turned to face the staff on the other side of the counter.

'I figure you understand now,' he said. 'So I want those goddam satchels out here now.'

Still in position at the bank's door Billy Dancer was giggling in his high voice at the senseless and bloody figure on the floor.

'Hey,' Benedict said, 'quit wetting your damn pants and watch the street, kid. You learned nothin' yet?'

Dancer scowled beneath his mask, but when Cagle turned to look at him as well he fell silent and turned stare out through the bank window. Nothing appeared to be happening out of the ordinary.

Minutes later the three bulky canvas satchels sat on the floor of the bank in front of Cagle. The three bank employees, the two tellers and the manager, were herded into the open vault and the door closed behind them.

'One bag each,' Cagle said. 'We walk out easy. Mount up and ride out slow and steady.'

They pulled down the masks covering their faces. Holstered their guns.

'What about him?' Dancer said, pointing at the man on the floor, lying in a pool of blood.

'He ain't about to do a damn thing,' Benedict said.

Cagle reached the door. 'Remember, nice and easy.'

He opened the door and stepped outside, Benedict behind and Dancer bringing up the rear.

They were on the boardwalk, the sun bright in their faces, when the voice reached them.

'This goes one of two ways. You put down the bags and raise your hands. Or I let go with this shotgun and we make a mess on the sidewalk. Your choice, boys. Just don't take too damn long, 'cause it's too hot to stand out here more than necessary.'

Cagle turned towards the voice and saw Bodie standing a few feet away. He was holding a double barrel piece that covered them all. Cagle held back the words forming in his throat. It wasn't the time to argue, especially with the man hunter. Bodie's reputation preceded him. There was no point making any argument with him. The man would as soon put a man down as exchange words, and as much as he felt angry at being taken so easily Vince Cagle knew there was little chance of walking away.

Billy Dancer chose the hard way. He dropped the satchel he was holding, screamed a mouthful of wild obscenities and went for his holstered gun. It was a foolish gesture, doomed from the start, and put all three of them in danger. Bodie could have easily tripped the shotgun's dual triggers and blown them to pieces. Instead he swung the hardwood butt of the shotgun and slammed it across the side of Dancer's face. The blow was brutal. It opened Dancer's face to the bone, blood streaming from the torn gash. Dancer went down hard, unconscious.

'Son of a bitch, I must be getting soft,' Bodie said. 'Now you pair toss those guns out on the street and pick up that kid.'

'He's not going to forget what you did,' Cagle said.

'It'll give him something to think about long cold nights in his cell,' Bodie said. 'Unless they hang you boys. Now let's get this over with. I been trailing you assholes for nigh on three weeks and kept missing you. Right now I want a bath and a hot meal, so let's get you tucked up nice and tight first.'

Armed men appeared from where they had been waiting for Bodie's signal and they took the prisoners and locked them up in Mesa's jail, prior to Bodie escorting them to Yuma, their trial, and sentencing to three years in the grim prison on the bluff overlooking the *muddy Colorado river.*

Walt Elkins had brought in a slick lawyer to defend his friends, and it was the man's persuasive words that had brought the prison sentence rather than a hang rope. It was a known fact that Cagle and his two partners had carried out a number of successful robberies, netting themselves a considerable amount of gold. Various agencies wanted that gold back, and the lawyer had bargained that being locked up in Yuma might persuade Cagle and company to give up the gold in exchange for a lessening of their long sentence. No guarantees from either side, but for a chance to regain possession of the gold the court and the agencies decided to take a chance. The presiding Judge who understood the fact that men who were hung were never going to come clean, and being a man with a reasonable expectation, put aside hanging and sentenced the trio to fifteen years — with a possible commutation if they gave up the gold cache.

Three years on, there was no compromise from the prisoners. They continued to serve their time. Elkins maintained the services of the lawyer and from time to time he was allowed to visit Yuma and discuss legal matters with Cagle. During those visits the lawyer would pass along messages from Elkins and take instruction from his client to pass back.

The most recent message from Cagle instructed Elkins to work out some method of breaking them free. They had bided their time for long enough. Cagle and Benedict and Dancer, seeing no other way, decided that three years was their limit and they wanted out.

So Elkins began to seek a way to break his friends free. He knew it was a nigh-on impossible matter. Prisoners didn't often escape from Yuma pen, but there was, he decided, a first time for everything.

And then he learned about the upcoming work party being set up from the guard in the Yuma saloon. The guard, one Cyrus Keno, Elkins had found out, was not just a drinker but a heavy gambler — and not a good one. The man owed money all over town. More money than he could ever afford. Guards working at the prison were not paid very well. The work was hard and ultimately not satisfying.

Elkins had already become Keno's close companion, working on the man and drawing him in with the long term intention of using the man. He sympathized with the man, bought him drinks and helped him out with money. When Keno let it slip a work crew was in the offing, Elkins upped the stakes. He offered Keno a large amount of money. Enough for Keno to clear his debts and have money in his pocket. All Keno had to do was make sure Cagle and company were on the work party. It turned out to be easier then Elkins had imagined. Keno, as a senior guard, was instrumental in setting up the prisoners who would be on the work party. He was also bossing the guards who would be overseeing the work. Once Keno conformed the set up, Elkins paid him half the money up front, with the rest to follow later.

He failed to inform Keno he wouldn't be getting the second payment. The intention was for Keno to be shot down along with the other guards on the work detail. A neat way of preventing the man from ever letting slip his connection with Elkins and the breakout that would follow.

The break went by the book. Elkins and his two men cut down the unsuspecting guard detail, Keno included, and the work party made their escape. Elkins lost one of his men. He and Teeler led Cagle, Benedict and Dancer to the waiting horses and they vanished . . .

4

'So let's get this done,' Cagle said. 'Sooner the better.' He glanced at Elkins. '*Walt?*'

Elkins nodded. 'Why not,' he said. 'I don't give a horse's ass if it is Bodie. If five of us can't take one man it's time we hung up our guns and took to our rockin' chairs.'

They broke camp and rode down off the high ground, taking the long way around to skirt Yuma and head south. Teeler had picked up talk while he was in town that Bodie would be scouting in that direction, because it was Cagle's old territory and he would start there.

'Let him catch our scent,' Cagle said. 'He caught us last time 'cause he figured out where we'd be. He'll ride his own trail, lookin' to catch us on home ground and by God I figure to let him do just that.'

'Ain't that asking for trouble?' Elkins said.

Dancer's shrill giggle sounded. 'He figures he's so smart,' he said. 'So we let him follow us until we turn right around and catch *him*. Ain't that right, Vince?'

'That's the general idea,' Cagle said. 'We lead him right where we want him.'

'Then we put that bastard right in the ground,' Dancer said.

'Too right,' Benedict said, for once agreeing with Dancer.

'We going south,' Elkins said, 'we'll need to grub up. Ain't enough now to keep us going long. We hit the desert country there's no places to buy supplies.'

Cagle considered that and nodded.

'You and Teeler fall back. Call on by Toomey's place. Pick up what we need.'

'We'll catch up later. Follow your tracks. We know about where you're going.'

Elkins nodded to Teeler and they

43

turned their horses around and rode out.

Though Elkins had the impression they were in the clear in truth it was the other way around. The man working for Elkins and shot during the ambush had been identified as being an accomplice of Elkins. Bodie had done his home-work and knowing now who had broken Cagle and company free Bodie had picked up the trail made by the group as they left the area. He doggedly followed as the gang moved around, then realized their roundabout route was taking them south, towards the desert country. Aware he was trailing five men Bodie stayed clear while he worked on how he might cut down the numbers.

His chance came when he picked up the tracks left by Elkins and Teeler as they separated from the others. He followed and it didn't take too long to figure they were heading for the small trading post close by. Elkins and Teeler would be going to pick up much needed supplies for the bunch before they rode south and into the solitary desert country. Bodie knew the area well and he used a route that got him to the trading post before Elkins and Teeler, tethering his horse out of sight at the back of the rambling building.

Elkins had imagined he was safe and did little to help himself, tying his horse at the peeling hitch rail and walking into the post, Teeler at his side. He only became aware something was off when he bellied up to the makeshift bar and ordered a couple of drinks. The man behind the bar gave himself away by showing distinct nervousness. His hand shook when he went to pour Elkins a shot of whisky and he spilled almost as much as he put in the glass.

Elkins' suspicious nature warned him and he leaned over the bar and grasped the trader's wrist.

'*What?*' he said. 'You're makin' me

figure things ain't right here. What you hiding?'

The trader, Toomey, yanked his hand free and stepped back.

'Ain't nothing to hide, friend,' he said in a voice less than convincing.

'*You think I'm stupid?*'

'If you're not,' someone said from the far side of the room, 'it's a pretty good impression.'

Elkin's turned away from the bar, searching for the source of the voice. And found it as Bodie stepped out of the shadows at the far end of the long room.

'Son of a bitch,' Elkins said. '*Bodie. How the hell did you find us?*'

'You pair leave a trail a blind man with a sack over his head could follow. You keep bad company too.'

'And you want to round 'em up again?'

'Caught Cagle and his crew once before. Governor at Yuma figured I'd have as good a chance second time around.'

'*The hell you will*,' Elkins yelled. 'Those are friends of mine and they ain't goin' back to that place. Sooner be dead . . . '

'That can be arranged.'

Out the corner of his eye Bodie saw Teeler easing off to the side, his hand already sliding in the direction of his holstered handgun.

Elkins reached across the bar and took the glass of whisky. He downed it with a quick motion of his left hand, and went for the Peacemaker on his hip with his shooting hand.

Toomey, watching, swore later that it all happened so quick he couldn't tell who was faster. All he recalled was the sudden burst of gunfire. It echoed loudly in the confines of the room. There were three close shots. Elkins' slug went wild as both of Bodie's hit. Elkins turned half around, his face taut with shock. A pair of fist-sized, bloody holes appeared in his back as Bodie's slugs cored into his body and blew out through his spine in a mist of bloody debris. He fell across the bar, his pistol bouncing from his hand, and slid along the edge of the counter until his body weight pulled him to the floor. He slammed face down.

Teeler had gone for his own weapon, sliding it free.

The second he fired at Elkins and before his body hit the floor, Bodie had changed position, turning sideways on. His Colt moved smoothly, tracking Teeler without pause and though the other man was fast, Bodie's Colt fired first. His single shot was on target, the solid lead slug thudding into Teeler's chest, knocking him back a step. Teeler's gun tilted skywards, his finger tripping the trigger and sending his lone shot up at the roof. Bodie raised the Colt and put a second slug into Teeler, placing it over the man's right eye and taking out the back of Teeler's skull on its exit. Teeler keeled over, body rigid and when he slammed down on the floor even Toomey felt the vibration.

The trader glanced at Bodie as he moved forward to stand over Elkins. Thin curls of smoke slid from the muzzle of the big Colt in his fist.

'He could have gone back to Yuma sitting his saddle instead of draped over it,' Bodie said.

'His choice,' Toomey, said.

Bodie glanced at the whisky glass, tipped on its side.

'That shot cost him dear.'

'You said it.'

Bodie pulled a twenty dollar coin from his pocket and spun it on the bar.

'That cover it?'

Toomey scooped up the coin, examined it.

'I'll get Hernandez to sew them up in burlap bags and put them in the cold cellar.'

'Make it soon. They won't stay fresh for long.'

'You got more urgent business?'

'Three more names on my list,' Bodie said.

'Do me a favor, Bodie,' Toomey

asked. 'Catch up with them a long way from here.'

He knew Bodie of old and was aware that the man hunter had a reputation for drawing trouble to him like a honey pot draws bees.

'You trying to hurt my feelings, Toomey?'

'No. Just asking nicely.'

'Way I see it those three are not going to be hanging around too close. When Elkins doesn't join up with them I'm figuring they'll keep right on moving.'

'Let's hope so. Bodie, you need any supplies?'

'Only a top-up for my canteen.'

'Help yourself. You know where the well is.'

Replacing the spent bullets, Bodie nodded and made his way outside, leaving Toomey to stare at the hole in the roof where Teeler's slug had passed through. A thin shaft of sunlight shone through and Toomey realized he needed to repair it. If it ever rained that hole was going to allow water in. Only a small matter but if he left it he'd have a wet patch grow. Toomey decided he'd get Hernandez repair it once he'd done putting Elkins to rest. One way and another the Mexican was going to have a busy day.

Out the corner of his eye Toomey caught sight of Bodie riding by the trading post window after collecting his horse from out back. He was glad to see the man go. As much as he liked him Toomey was always relieved when Bodie moved on.

'*Buena suerte, amigo.*'

He had a feeling Bodie was going to need it.

5

Bodie tracked the three riders, using Elkins' trail to where he had parted company with his friends. The ground was dry and there was no wind, so the hoof prints had remained clear. The trail led south and west. Not somewhere Bodie would have chosen. There was little ahead, save for barren desert land. An unquestionably hostile environment. Sand and rock. Scant vegetation and with a scarcity of water unless a man knew the location of the few sources. Bodie had ridden here on other occasions and he didn't take to it. Right now he had no choice because that was where Cagle, Benedict and Dancer were riding. He found himself wondering why.

A couple of hours later he found out why the hard way . . .

* * *

. . . his horse shot from under him. Canteen punctured so he had no water. There was no doubt they had him at a disadvantage. On foot and forced to maintain his distance, Bodie had been presented with a single option.

He called himself every kind of fool. He had allowed himself to be drawn into following them, without figuring it was what they wanted. And his lack of concentration had betrayed him. If Bodie had been the kind to make excuses he could have blamed his mistake on being tired from the long ride to catch up with his quarry. Too long with little sleep. Pushing himself too hard. Another man might have done that. Bodie didn't. He had no one else to blame but himself and he was paying for his slip up now. He had been eager to catch up with Cagle and his partners. Maybe too eager and it had edged him towards being a touch careless.

So all he could do was put it behind him and do what was needed to pull himself out of trouble. It was not in Bodie's nature to back away. But given he was no man's fool and able to assess what would be in his best interest for the present, Bodie had accepted the way it was.

He was unable to get to his rifle. It was trapped beneath the dead horse's bulk, the same with half his saddle-bags. He dropped his hand to his revolver. Found the holster empty. The heavy Colt had slipped from leather as he had fallen from his horse. He spotted where it lay a few feet away, close enough, but with Billy Dancer waiting with his rifle those few feet made all the difference.

'Not your best day, son,' Bodie muttered. 'Next time take a breath and think hard and long before you go in.'

He scanned his surroundings. The empty Arizona desert, a spread of raw land where little grew and the heat of a pitiless sun turned the area into a place men avoided if there was a choice.

Nothing moved in his sight. He became aware of the hot sun on his back, penetrating his shirt. The soft drift of the desert breeze that picked up sand and threw it back and forth. Already his lips and mouth were dry again. What little water he'd got from his draining canteen was already losing its effect. If he stayed where he was the relentless heat would work on him until every last drop of moisture was sucked out of him. If he didn't get to where he could find cover and water Billy Dancer wouldn't need to use up his ammunition. The desert would kill Bodie as sure as any bullet.

'*Hey, Bodie, warm day, huh?*'

Dancer couldn't resist his taunt. Taking pleasure from Bodie's discomfort.

'I got an extra canteen here, bounty man. You want some? Just step out and I'll think about sharing.'

Thanks, Billy, Bodie thought. He ignored Dancer.

He had positioned Dancer from his

voice. Dancer was behind a jagged line of shallow rocks jutting up from the sand some thirty feet away. The knowledge didn't remove the threat but at least it showed where Dancer was.

Bodie checked his Colt again. Measured the distance. In truth not that far, but with Dancer covering him it might as well have been a country mile. In the end Bodie had no choice. The Colt represented his only chance to defend himself. If he didn't do something . . .

With his mind made up Bodie moved. There was no point stretching it out. Waiting wasn't going to bring his revolver closer. He dug in his boots and lunged forward, over the dead horse, his body straining as he reached out for the gun.

His move must have caught Dancer by surprise and it took the concealed shooter seconds to recover.

Bodie's outstretched fingers were reaching for the Colt when Dancer's rifle crashed. The slug smacked into the ground inches away . . . there was a pause as Dancer levered another shell into the breech.

Bodie was almost there, resisting the urge to think about a slug slamming into his body. He concentrated on reaching the revolver.

The second shot came.

Bodie felt the slug tear at his left arm, jerking it aside. He made the final effort and closed his fingers over the hot butt of the pistol, yanking it to him. His fingers closed tight and he pulled the weapon around, thumbing back the hammer and putting a shot in the direction of Dancer's hiding place. The moment he fired Bodie dragged himself back behind cover, hearing yet another shot, forcing himself up and over the horse's bulk. The slug pounded at the carcass as Bodie dropped out of sight. He landed on his back, panting from the exertion. Sweat beaded his face.

Dancer opened up with a hard volley. Driving shot after shot at the dead horse. Bodie managed a thin smile at Dancer's rage.

Go ahead, Billy, waste your ammunition.

He felt the rising pain from his arm and put down the Colt so he could check the wound. He rolled up the blood-sodden sleeve and exposed the damage. The slug had torn a raw and ragged trench in the flesh, just above his elbow. It hadn't damaged the bone but the wound was bleeding freely and the flesh was open and raw.

'Dancer, you son of a bitch,' Bodie said.

He used his knife to hack at his shirt, cutting the right arm free and used it to wrap tightly around the wound. He sliced off a thin strip as a tie, using his free hand and his teeth to secure it. It took him a few attempts before he managed to get it in place. He was the first to admit it was clumsy and it wasn't the best way to treat an open wound. There wasn't much he could about it at the moment. By the time he'd done the arm was giving him considerable pain. Bodie figured if he could feel it at least he was still alive.

He picked up the Colt again. Took a little time to scan the surrounding terrain. With it being reasonably flat he was able to see a distance. He was looking for Dancer's partners.

Vince Cagle and Tobe Benedict would be somewhere nearby. They might even be riding in now, alerted by the shooting.

Bodie didn't fancy letting himself become trapped by all three. He needed to get clear. Allow himself some breathing space. To do that he had to break away from his current position. Which meant doing something about Billy Dancer.

But what?

He needed to work out something fast. Time wasn't on his side.

6

In the end Bodie realized he wasn't going to be allowed any fancy tricks to get him out of this bind. Dancer was waiting and Bodie had no magic solution to take the man off his back. It was no time for debating the issue.

He took a quick look around. Twenty yards at his back Bodie spotted a slight rise in the ground. A low ridge that ran east to west. It might be nothing more than an irregular formation and he had no way of knowing what lay beyond it. It could, he imagined, be the lip of a dried-out water course. If that was so it would most likely provide a shallow gulley he could use for cover. He also accepted it might also be a ridge in the earth with nothing beyond. Bodie figured whatever it offered it had to an improvement on a dead horse. Flies were already converging on the carcass and before long it would start to smell.

He checked the Colt. Spun the cylinder to make sure it was clear. Reaching down he wedged the big knife firm in its sheath. When he'd fallen from his horse he had lost his hat. It lay close by and he grabbed it now, jamming it tight on his head. Bodie turned, his back against the horse and stared at the ridge. Took a couple of deep breaths. Then he gathered his legs under him and pushed to his feet, digging in hard with his boots, and took off in a weaving run.

Good goddamn this had better work, he told himself.

Dancer's first shot whacked into the ground feet away. It kicked up a sandy geyser. Bodie kept moving, knowing there would be more shots. He moved left and right, presenting a difficult target. He resisted the urge to look back, even pushing away the need to return fire. Dancer had the advantage using a long gun. Even so the next couple of shots were way off target and

Bodie was beginning to feel Dancer was not such a good shot anyhow. By the law of averages the man would eventually get lucky. Bodie put on a spurt, his eyes fixed on the ridge ahead.

On the periphery of his vision he caught movement off to his right. Blurred at first but quickly taking on form. A pair of riders coming in his direction, spurring their mounts hard as they angled towards him.

Cagle and Benedict.

It had to be them.

Bodie saw the ridge line coming up. Increased his speed and cleared the ridge, taking himself over in a full dive. He had the impression of a steep slope dropping away from him. Heard the rattle of multiple shots that hit the ridge behind him. He slammed face down, his momentum carrying him forward, raising a cloud of sandy dust in his wake. The slope ran down at a steep angle and Bodie felt his own body weight pulling along. He hit bottom, feeling the scrape of hard, dry earth under him. His hat flew from his head again and this time he had no opportunity to snatch it up again.

Bodie twisted round, coming up on one knee, saw movement on the rim of the bank above him.

Billy Dancer, face twisted in anger as he angled his rifle down at Bodie . . . who snapped up his Colt, hammer back and finger against the trigger. The revolver fired flame and smoke. Dancer let out a screech as the .45 slug slammed into his left shoulder. The heavy lead slug punched a bloody exit hole, the force knocking Dancer back from the rim and dumping him on his knees. He dropped his rifle, clasping a hand to his shoulder, pain from the wound kicking in seconds later.

The moment he dropped the trigger Bodie pushed to his feet and turned, heading along the gulley. He needed to gain distance. Cover from Cagle and Benedict. Wounding Dancer might have bought him some time, but he wasn't about to count on it lasting long.

Dancer's partners were not going to allow him much freedom from pursuit.

A rifle fired behind him, the sound hard in the wide-open desert landscape. The slug kicked up dust well away from Bodie. He figured someone was firing from the back of a moving horse. Not the best position for accurate shooting.

As Bodie followed the natural curve of the gully, taking him briefly out of sight of his pursuers, a quick thought came into his mind.

Desert landscape.

He was moving further into the desert. The desolate, sun-scorched wasteland where heat and the lack of water could kill a man as easily as a rifle slug. Cagle and Benedict were going to know that and they would make sure he wouldn't be able to turn about and circle his way around them.

Like it or not Bodie had to keep moving south, hoping to gain distance, but at the same time taking himself into the desert . . .

7

'*Son of a bitch, we damn sure got him now,*' Tobe Benedict crowed. 'He's running south. Right into the desert. If we don't put a bullet in him, he'll burn up more'n likely.'

'Never no mind about Bodie,' Dancer yelled. 'He put a goddamn slug in me. *Jesus, it hurts, damnit.* What about that?'

He was down on the ground, making enough noise to raise the dead, and spilling blood.

Vince Cagle was kneeling beside him, trying to get a clear view of the bloody wound.

'Sit still, Billy, you asshole. How can I do anything with you jiggin' all over?'

'But it hurts, Vince, god it hurts.'

'That's because you were dumb enough to let Bodie shoot you.'

'Hey, Vince, you want me to trail after him?' Benedict said. 'See where he's going?'

'You got a mind to then just do it,' Cagle said. 'Not likely he's going to walk out of sight.'

'Guess so. But he might turn about and circle us.'

'Make sure he don't,' Cagle said. 'Do I have to do all the damn thinking for this outfit?'

Benedict checked his rifle, replaced the loads he'd used earlier. He took up his reins and eased his horse away.

Ignoring Dancer's continued moaning, Cagle crossed to his ground reined horse and opened his saddlebags. He pulled out a shirt and a flat bottle of liquor. He pulled out the knife tucked in his boot and cut away Dancer's shirt from around the wound. The entry hole was neat but where the bullet had emerged from his shoulder the flesh was ragged and torn. The damaged flesh had formed a pulpy mass, still bleeding.

'Lucky it didn't break no bone,' Cagle said.

'Oh, I guess that's okay then,' Dancer said.

'Billy, you got one hell of a sour disposition.'

'*Yeah?* Well, you get yourself shot and see if it cheers you up.'

Cagle cut the shirt into wide strips. Made a thick pad from more of the cloth. He pulled the stopper from the bottle and took a quick slug. He held out the bottle.

'You want some?'

'Hell, no, I don't want no liquor.'

'Suit yourself, Billy,' Cagle said and poured some of the raw liquor over the entry and exit wounds.

Dancer squealed as the alcohol burned its way into the wounds. Ignoring the noise Cagle placed the folded pad over the exit wound and pressed down, closing the bloody mound of flesh.

'*Goddam you to hell*,' Dancer howled. 'What you do that for?'

'Keep the wound clean,' Cagle said, fashioning a crude bandage around Dancer's arm and shoulder.

'You like to burned my shoulder.'

'Billy, shut your damn mouth. It's like I'm dealing with a woman here.'

Dancer didn't make a complaint this time. When Cagle looked he saw the younger man had passed out.

'Smartest thing you done today, Billy.'

He finished tying off the bandage, then sat back and took another mouthful from the bottle, and got to wondering where Benedict had got to.

★ ★ ★

The man called Silverbuck had gone to where his horse was tethered. From the packed saddle bag pouch he pulled out a wrapped object. He opened the soft cloth to expose a lovingly cared for pair of binoculars. The brass and leather was clean and unmarked. He had actually *bought* the instrument a number of years back and had found it useful when he was tracking someone. The powerful magnification allowed him to spy on someone from a long way off. He hung the binoculars around his neck by the retaining strap and made his way back to his vantage point. He took one of his canteens with him and took a slow sip as he settled down again. He raised the glasses and focused on the distant ridge line where Bodie had disappeared.

He checked out the two men crouched near the gulley. The one Bodie had wounded was stretched out, his shoulder bandaged by one of his partners. The third man was some distance further on, mounted and carrying a rifle. He was following the line of the gulley where Bodie had taken cover. Silverbuck could see a thin mist of dust from the man hunter's passing, but he failed to actually see the man himself.

Silverbuck sat back on his heels, considering his next move. He decided to stay out of sight for the moment. If he exposed himself too quickly he would have these men to take on as well as Bodie. As much as he wanted the Stalker, Silverbuck had no intention of adding to his own problems.

He could feel a growing ache in his arm. It troubled him from time to time, giving him pain. Even thought it had healed in the bone there was a lingering problem with the nerve endings that had been damaged in the limb and there were times when Silverbuck suffered for long periods. At least here in the hot desert the pain was bearable. When it was cold the pain became stronger, a nagging ache that refused to go away. During those times the anger in him grew hot and his need for vengeance against Bodie rose until he could have screamed in his fury. He found he was stroking his fingers across the ridged neck scar. Of all his wounds it was the one he hated Bodie for more than any other. He had survived the brutal cut but in the event he had lost the ability to speak as he should. He had lived when he should have died, yet now he was barely able to communicate and it was that which pained him more than anything.

Damn you, Bodie, I will make you suffer a living hell before I end your life.

He made the promise in the name of *Ussen*, the god of the Apache — not someone Silverbuck acknowledged very often, but on this occasion he meant it.

★ ★ ★

Benedict had pushed his horse along the ridge, eyes searching for Bodie. He knew the others would join him once Cagle had the kid sorted. Dancer getting himself shot was going to slow them down. Too damned eager to prove himself, that was Billy Dancer. He was lucky Bodie hadn't managed a killing shot. If he'd had time that *would* have happened. The man hunter didn't waste time on wounding. Benedict kept reminding himself about that. Whatever happened out here no one was going back to Yuma unless it was over the back of a horse. This was a one-way ride.

Drawing rein Benedict raised in his saddle.

Where the hell had Bodie gone?

He followed the meandering line of the gulley. Saw nothing. Heard nothing. It was like the man had vanished. Benedict looked across the opposite ridge. If Bodie wasn't in the gulley he had to have climbed the far side and moved on.

'Okay, you son of a bitch, we can all play games,' Benedict said.

He rode down into the gulley and up the far bank, sitting and scanning the surrounding landscape. The desert spread out ahead of him. Silent and empty. Heat waves shimmering. A desert breeze disturbing the sand. Benedict turned his horse full circle.

Nothing. It was like he was the only man alive. He tipped back his hat and ran his sleeve across his face. The heat was vicious. It hammered down on a man, giving no relief.

It brought back memories of his time in Yuma. The endless hours in the cramped and stinking cells with no escape from the crippling temperature. The unforgiving tedium of the days and the chill nights. Bad food. Guards who would beat a man as soon as look at him. Benedict still had scars on his back from being beaten. Hell on earth, they called Yuma Pen, and that was what it was. A man was punished every day he spent in that place. Well, Tobe Benedict was out now, and he was never going back. Once they had settled with Bodie, the three of them were going to get as far away from Arizona as they could. It would have been easy to do that now. Simply ride on and forget the prison and Bodie. But that wasn't going to happen. Benedict and Cagle and Dancer had a reckoning to settle first. None of them would feel content until Bodie was lying at their feet. Even if they had walked away Bodie would stay on their trail, hunting them down. It was in his nature. The only way they would ever feel totally free would be when he was dead. When they had paid him back for the three years they had lost in that damned prison.

And with the man hunter dead they could collect the gold waiting for them. The bank at Mesa had been their final robbery, the one where the three had been caught, sentenced and jailed. If they had given up the gold they had previously stolen they might have received lesser sentences, but Cagle, Benedict and Dancer had remained silent about it. They figured to do their time, then retrieve the gold coins and take off with it. After rotting in Yuma, as Cagle had said, they had earned the money.

Breaking out had seemed a good idea at the time. Having Bodie appear on the scene had been a bonus. Cagle had seen it as a sign things were on the up for them.

Kill Bodie.

Collect their cash.

Ride on.

Benedict wet his lips from his canteen. Swallowed a little more water.

Already the perspective had changed. Okay, they had Bodie on the run. But Billy had been wounded and Bodie had vanished.

Son of a bitch.

He was on foot. No water. Being pushed into the desert, and he still managed to give them the slip.

Benedict leaned forward, eyes fixed on a distant spot. He was certain he had seen movement. To the south and off to the west. He stared until his eyes ached. The heat haze made it hard to be certain. It could have been a man — then Benedict wasn't so sure. The shimmering disturbance of the air made it hard to be certain. Benedict squeezed his eyes shut, blinked to clear his vision, then took another look.

Nothing this time.

His eyes must have been playing tricks on him.

Even so Bodie was out there. And Tobe Benedict didn't give up easy. He urged his horse forward. *Keep looking over your shoulder, Bodie, 'cause I'm still here and still coming for you.*

8

Bodie lay in the scant shadow of the tangled catclaw, his body stretched out full length in the shallow dip. He had pulled the soft sand of the hollow over him so he was partially buried. From where he lay he could see the mounted figure of Tobe Benedict as the man took his time checking out the area. The man *was* taking his time, most likely aware that Bodie had to be somewhere close. It hadn't been long for the man hunter to have moved out of sight, so Benedict had to be figuring he was still close. Just hidden.

Most likely watching. And waiting.

* * *

It was uncomfortable where Bodie lay. The ground under him was hot and the high sun beat down with unrelenting ferocity. The scant shade offered by the catclaw did nothing to reduce the sun. Even the Colt in Bodie's hand was hot, sweat forming on his palm where it gripped the butt.

He admitted to himself that Cagle and his partners had caught him between a rock and a hard place. Pushing him south, into the desert, had been a smart move as far as they were concerned. Nothing ahead of him but more sun scorched emptiness and between Bodie and safety, Cagle, Benedict and Dancer. Not much of a choice, but it was the best offer he was likely to get.

Following the tracks after dealing with Elkins had brought Bodie to his current situation and he couldn't blame anyone but himself. He'd been too eager to catch up with the three and he had admittedly lowered his guard. That was then, this was now, and no point feeling sorry for himself. So he had walked into an impasse and all that was open to him was getting out of it.

Bodie focused on Benedict. The man was too far for a shot from the Colt. Well out of range. Bodie thought of the rifle he'd had to leave pinned under his dead horse. Having that in his hands would have leveled the odds.

He watched as Benedict trailed his horse along the rim of the gully, still searching. Benedict was staying where he was, keeping beyond the range of Bodie's revolver. His position allowed him to scope out the landscape without presenting himself as an easy target. If Bodie did move he would be seen soon enough. A dark figure against the pale sand. So he stayed where he was, biding his time until Benedict tired of standing guard. He saw the man take another drink from his canteen. It reminded Bodie of his own thirst. His mouth was parched, sour-tasting. He couldn't even raise any saliva and Bodie didn't try because that would have hurt his throat. What was maddening was the fact there was a water source close by, he realized. No more than a few miles off to the west.

Pinto Wells it was called. Created eons ago during volcanic eruptions that had pushed up from below the ground, where hot lava had spewed out and flowed across the surface of the earth, forming as it cooled into a series of rocky formations. Countless years had weathered the hardened crust and sand storms had smoothed the dark rock. And in time water from a deep underground source had broken through. A natural water course, where the constant pressure of the stream forced it to the surface, finding its way through the fractured rock, the precious liquid bubbled it way out to fill the rock pans. The flow of water had worn the rocks smooth over eons. Through the long years animals and man had used the place. Pinto Wells, as it had been named, was one of the few constant water sources. Many watering holes depended on rainfall to replenish them. Pinto Wells never ran out. There were very few of these natural places and Bodie had learned to pinpoint their existence. Right now he might as well have been a thousand miles from the spot. As long as he was being covered by Benedict and company that water offered nothing more than a prize that might turn out to be well beyond his reach.

Bodie felt the tug of a rising wind. Lifted his head and felt it ruffle his hair. Over the next few minutes that soft breeze increased and started to pick up dust and sand. It was coming in from the southwest. Bodie checked in that direction and saw the distant, approaching swirl of a sand storm. As it swept in his direction it was picking up loose detritus. With each passing minute the strength increased and the density of the cloud increased. The first of the sandy particles reached Bodie. He knew that it might be a swift pass. The power of the wind sweeping over him and vanishing in minutes. But during that time he would be pretty well hidden from Benedict. It was a chance for him to move. To clear the area and find himself better cover. A slim chance. Maybe his only chance, but for Bodie it was worth taking. He also knew the storm might take its time, the blast of hot air remaining for some long period.

Bodie checked the position of the sun. It was more or less directly overhead. Noon. The hottest part of the day. From there it would begin its slow descent into the west. It would take a long time and the heat would remain. With the coming of the sand storm the desert area would be at its worst. Bodie would use that to his advantage.

He checked back to where Benedict still sat his horse, hunched over in his saddle, with his neckerchief already pulled over the lower part of his face against the intrusive dust.

Persistent son of a bitch, Bodie thought.

Over the next few minutes the dust cloud grew more intense and now Bodie couldn't even see Benedict. He figured this was a good as it was going to get. He slid out of cover, shrugging off the layer of sand and pushed to his feet. He pushed the Colt inside his shirt to prevent it becoming clogged. Head down he leaned into the wind and moved off. He wasn't far from being blind. The storm was in its full fury now, the thick rolls of sand pounding him as he pushed through. The sand peppered him, stinging any exposed flesh and Bodie shielded his eyes with one hand. It was hard work moving forward, the sand dragging at his feet, soft underfoot, making each step harder than the one previous. He found he was having to breathe through his nose. If he opened his mouth it would take in more sand than air.

He lost track of time. Didn't even attempt to work out how long he'd been stumbling through the enveloping fog of dust and sand. He just kept slogging forward, checking the sky and occasionally catching a glimpse of the sun and making sure he hadn't veered off track. As long as he kept it ahead he knew he was moving directly west.

Staying on course was all that mattered right now. He needed to reach the distant *tinajas*, because that was where he would find water. Pinto Wells. If he didn't reach there, the three men pursuing him might find the desert had claimed him before their bullets found him. A grin formed on Bodie's parched lips. He was caught in the middle, between two unfavorable endings.

He could die from dehydration — or from lead poisoning.

Bodie didn't see any advantage in either, so he made up his mind to positively reject them both.

9

Silverbuck saw the storm long before it arrived. He left his vantage place and took his horse to a sheltered spot where he sat out the wind and clouds of sand within the rock walls of a deep fissure. He waited with the inborn patience that was part of his heritage. He may have only been a half-blood but he carried inside him the capacity to exist with the land and not fight it. Live *with* the land. Become as one with it. Take what good it had to offer and not resist when it presented its harder face. It was the only way because man was never stronger than the land. If he defied it the land would eat him up and spit out his bones.

Bodie would put himself against the storm, Silverbuck knew, because he had little choice in the matter. It would offer him a chance to break away from the three following him. The *Pinda Lickoyi* was no fool. He was hard and a survivor and he would not give in.

The men chasing him were driven by thoughts of revenge. They would let their anger direct them along Bodie's trail and if the desert did not destroy them they would follow Bodie until *he* turned on them — which he would.

This would all resolve itself once the storm blew itself out, so there was little need to hurry to catch up. With these thoughts Silverbuck remained within his refuge, the fury of the storm blowing around him and tended to his weapons, his horse close by, the both of them protected by the deep fissure in the rocks. While he waited he considered the way things were.

The *Pinda Lickoyi* man hunter, Bodie, would use the storm to escape from his pursuers. He knew the land and Silverbuck saw that the man would make for the *tinajas* at Pinto Wells that lay to the west. The three men chasing him might also know of the place and they would follow. If the fates allowed they would all converge on the rock pans and that would be the place they would try to kill Bodie.

That would also allow Silverbuck his moment of vengeance. It was an inevitability that Pinto Wells would become the final battleground when he came upon the place.

Silverbuck completed his cleaning of his weapons. Using a slightly oiled cloth from his ammunition pouch he carefully cleaned the Colt revolver, taking out the big .45 caliber bullets and wiping them, then did the same with the six chambers and mechanism, making sure everything was clean. He checked the action and when he was satisfied he reloaded the revolver and placed it back in the holster around his waist. He carried out the same procedure with the Winchester rifle. The adapted weapon could be hung across his back by the plaited rawhide sling and brought quickly into play. The barrel and stock had been cut down to create a short-range, but effective weapon. Silverbuck preferred close-up situations rather than killing from long distance, so the reduced range of the Winchester suited his needs. The ammunition he used, for both pistol and rifle, had been marked by deep cross-cuts in the soft lead slugs. On impact the deformed slugs would spread and create deep, ugly wounds. A way to determine any hits Silverbuck made would increase the stopping power. It was a sure way to make certain his victims were less likely to walk away from an encounter. Silver-buck's armament was completed by the broad-bladed, razor-edged knife he carried. The original knife he had owned now belonged to Bodie. He had used it on Silverbuck, slicing open the breed's own throat and leaving him for dead. Silverbuck had sought out and replaced the knife with another, identical weapon. Holding it in his hand Silverbuck was determined to pay back Bodie in kind and make sure that he was successful when he cut open the *Pinda Lickoyi's* throat . . .

Silverbuck sat back, satisfied he had everything ready. He unconsciously reached up a hand to stroke the ridged scar that stretched across his throat.

You can run, Bodie, but you cannot hide from me now I have found you. My time is coming and I will kill you. And even if the Pinda Lickoyi who follow kill you first I will make you alive again so you will die at my hand.

Silverbuck, who had been Massai, made that vow and offered it to *Ussen*, the God of the Apache.

Now it was written. And any promise made to *Ussen* could not be broken.

★   ★   ★

'I know where that son is heading,' Cagle said. 'The *tinajas* west of here. Only just come to me. Pinto Wells. That's where he's going.'

'How the hell do you work that out?' Dancer said. He was still in a lot of

89

pain, weak, but determined to sit his saddle when they moved on. 'There's a whole lot of country out there to choose from for Christ's sake.'

'Figure it out, Billy,' Cagle said. 'The man's on foot. No water since you put a slug through his canteen. And you said you caught him with one of your shots. So the feller isn't in the best position to go wandering too far into the desert.'

'No other place he can go,' Benedict agreed. 'He'll need water. Badly. In this heat he's going to have a mouth drier than a witch's tit. He don't get water all we'll find is his body shriveled up and baked to a crisp. I got no likin' for the man, but he knows the country and if I'm guessing right he'll know all the watering holes around. And Pinto Wells is closest.'

'Tobe's right,' Cagle said. 'Call Bodie what you will but he's no man's fool. If anyone can walk through this desert and come out the other side it's Bodie.'

'Jesus, listening to you pair it's like you fell in love with the *hombre*.'

'I think you're set agin' him 'cause he put a bullet in you,' Benedict said, a thin smile edging his mouth.

'And you'd be damned right,' Dancer said.

They were sitting out the heart of the storm, sheltering in the gully, backs to the clouds of gritty sand and dust, horses pulled in close. Each man had his blanket pulled around his head and shoulders to keep out the gritty dust that filtered down. As eager as they were to pick up the chase none of them even considered venturing out while the storm raged. There would be time enough to start out once it abated. If they had learned one lesson while in Yuma prison it was patience. The ability to accept the moment and wait. Being in the cells behind those grim walls had made them more than aware that raging against the inevitable was a negative pursuit. As willful as banging their heads against the stone enclosures. Better to stay heads down and let things roll by. When the storm moved on, as it eventually would, then they could fork their saddles and move out.

Bodie was on foot. Hampered by the same storm that was holding them back, he would not have covered much ground, and it stood to reason they would be able to close the distance much faster once they were able to ride again.

Even Billy Dancer saw the sense in waiting, thought it grated. He wanted his chance against Bodie. The opportunity to empty his gun in the man hunter. That was going to be something he would enjoy because he really owed the man big time. Squatting against the slope of the gully, hunched over in his blanket, listening to the howl of the storm and feeling the gritty sand slapping against him, Dancer envisaged killing Bodie. He still felt weak and sick, his shoulder giving him constant pain, but Dancer let his imagination run free. Billy Dancer harbored grudges. Never let a personal slight be forgotten. He allowed them to fester and become dark, ugly things that skittered around the corners of his mind until they burst free in bouts of reckless violence. And what Bodie had done was still fresh enough in Dancer's mind to keep him keyed up and able to sit out the pain in his shoulder. He pulled his blanket closer around him, blocking out the light and brooded in silence while he waited . . .

10

Determined as he was to reach Pinto Wells, Bodie quickly realized he was going to have to ease up. The sheer force of the sandstorm he was walking into made movement difficult. Physical strength was not enough to counter the buffeting and Bodie was pushed to his knees on a number of occasions. He fought to gain his feet again each time, aware that even his power to resist was being sorely tested. Time became an abstract thing. He had no notion how long he'd been walking, leaning into the wind, attempting to keep the dust and sand from overwhelming him.

Bodie stumbled and fell again. Felt the sheer power of the wind push him sideways until he was driven against something hard and unyielding. It took him moments to realize he was jammed against a jutting rock formation and as he felt around it he located a number of boulders rising from the desert's surface. Accepting he wasn't going to gain much headway until the full force of the storm eased off Bodie worked his way into the shelter provided by the rocks. As he eased himself into the gap he felt the pressure of the storm becoming reduced. The rocks were diverting it, giving him some degree of protection. Bodie took the opportunity to use the cover. He brushed at the sand in his hair. Cleared it from his face and eyes. There was little choice left to him now. Like it or not he was going to need to sit out the storm. Wait until he was able to move on freely.

He listened to the hissing rattle of sand against the sheltering rocks. The moan of the wind. And he thought about Pinto Wells and the cool, sweet water rippling over the smooth worn rock pans. A bad train of thought. It only made him realize how thirsty he was. His mouth and throat parched. The skin of his face and hands scoured by the wind-driven sand.

Not the best day he'd ever had, Bodie decided, and it wasn't promising to get any better. He'd lost his horse, his possessions and water supply. And caught a bullet wound in his arm — which was still offering him a nagging pain. All in all something of a loss.

Regardless of the downturn Bodie had no intention of quitting. The momentary lapse in resolve had come and gone. If there was any truth to be told Bodie was not a man to step away from any situation. He hadn't built his reputation on walking away. Any of the men he'd gone after could affirm to that — if they survived and were still alive after he caught up to them. Doggedness was one of his qualities. A deserved accolade because Bodie never, ever, gave up.

Cagle and Benedict and Dancer might be the ones doing the chasing at the moment — but the situation would be turned around once Bodie found his place to make his stand.

And Pinto Wells was as good a place as any.

If the situation change before he reached the *tinajas* Bodie would handle that as well. He had learned a long time ago that in his profession being flexible was a handy attribute. Confrontations couldn't always be stage-managed. People had the habit of doing the opposite to what was hoped for and expected.

Easing the Colt from under his shirt Bodie checked it over. He worked the hammer and spun the cylinder, making sure it was still running free. He found nothing to worry over. He kept his weapons in tip-top condition because he depended on them to work at any given moment without having to have concerns. While he did that he kept an ear open for the sound of the sandstorm, listening for any easing in its strength.

That didn't happen for almost an hour.

Bodie picked up on the drop in pressure. The slackening of the depth of sound. He waited it out. Peering from behind his sheltering rocks he saw the blue sky showing through the storm haze and over the following half hour the wind dropped to a whisper, the choking swirl of sand fading. He slid out from behind the shelter of rock and stood, easing the stiffness from his body. Over his shoulder he saw the dust cloud moving away from him, leaving only the seemingly ever-present slight breeze that hung over the desert.

Checking the position of the still-high sun Bodie fixed his position for Pinto Wells. He was on track. Still a distance away but on track. The thought of the cool water in the rock pools gave him the strength to move out.

He hadn't forgotten who was behind him. Knew that once the storm blew itself completely away they would be moving as well. He dropped the .45 caliber Peacemaker back into his holster. As Bodie strode out he shook off the remaining sand from his clothing. He still had to put up with the hot sun. Nothing he could do about that and he was well aware it would burn away at his reserves of stamina over the next few hours.

He also knew it would not stop him. Come hell or high water he was going to reach Pinto Wells and wait for Vince Cagle and his crew. When they did show up the tranquil peace of the watering hole was going to be well and truly disturbed.

* * *

Silverbuck rode out from his sanctuary as the storm slid away to the east. He led his horse out from cover, checked it over then mounted up. He rode slowly down in the direction of the gully where the three *Pinda Lickoyi* had waited out the storm. With the ease of the Apache he followed them, knowing they would never see him. They rode without skill, leaving a trail he could follow without even trying, so he could stay well back from them. Tracking them was easy. An Apache child could have followed them. They would lead him to Bodie and never know it. And when the dying time came Bodie would be there at Pinto Wells, the rocks at his back and a flaming gun in his hand.

It would be worth the watching. Seeing the three Americans die by Bodie's hand, leaving the way open for Silverbuck to finish what he had come for. It was coming the way he wanted.

Silverbuck stroked his horse's neck.

'We will have our finish,' he said. '*Enjuh. Enjuh.*'

Good. It is well.

And he gave his thanks to *Ussen.*

★   ★   ★

'*Godawful sand,*' Dancer complained. 'I even got it up my butt.'

'Yeah?' Benedict said. 'Now seein' as you talk out of your ass most of the time, Billy, that ain't no surprise.'

Benedict chuckled at his own joke. Dancer scowled at his back and for one wild moment dropped his hand to the butt of his holstered revolver.

'*Billy* . . . ' Cagle said softly, his horse alongside the younger man's.

'He shouldn't say . . . '

'You know Tobe. Allus likes to make his little joke. Don't let him get to you, boy.'

Dancer sank down in his saddle, favoring his bandaged shoulder. His normally lean face looked haggard. He chanced a look at Cagle.

'One day,' he whispered. 'It'll come.'

'Long as it ain't today, Billy, 'cause we got better things to do. Just think on.'

They were moving slowly across the heat seared desert landscape. They didn't push their mounts, knowing that would be fatal. As eager as they were to catch up with Bodie, pushing their horses too hard could leave them on foot as well.

In the far distance they could see the

dark line of low mountain peaks shimmering through the heat waves. Behind them just the mark of their passing in the sand. Only occasionally did they see scant vegetation emerging from the desert. Scraps of hardy galleta grass. Some ironwood. The desert during its dry time, which was most of it, barely sustained plant life. Yet when it rained, even for a short time, the desert bloomed. Green plants. The odd flower. Then the desert took on a change.

For Cagle, Benedict and Dancer, there was little time to appreciate the state of the landscape. Only a few thoughts dominated their minds.

Finding Bodie.

Killing Bodie.

Then moving on to reclaim their hidden cache of stolen gold.

A simple enough plan.

Simple in thought, but executing it might not be so easy.

Both Cagle and Benedict, as good as they were, reminded themselves who they were going up against.

Bodie.

The Stalker.

A man hunter with a set of skills that set him apart from others of his kind. To disregard the man's ability to survive would be a mistake. A fatal mistake. To face Bodie without regard his reputation was akin to walking in blind.

So Cagle and Benedict rode with those thoughts.

Billy Dancer, young, full of his own immortality, approached Pinto Wells with a different attitude. He saw his partners as men on the cusp. Hard, yes. Uncompromising in their way, but these days always tempered with too much caution. He saw them as starting to lose their edge. He rode with them because they had taught him a lot. Had passed along the knowledge gained from years on the trail. Even during their time in Yuma they had kept together. But Dancer found he was moving away from their way. He saw his time with them coming to a close. He had his life ahead and with his skill with his gun he saw good times ahead. Dancer wanted more than life on the move. Forever looking over his shoulder. Times were changing and Dancer wanted to go along with that change. Not spend the rest of his life on the dodge. With his share of the money he could step up in the world. Go places. Meet better people.

It was one of the main reasons why he stayed with Cagle. He needed the man to lead him to the hidden money. Cagle was the only one who knew where the cache was.

But first he needed to finish this thing with Bodie. Along with the others Dancer had lost three years of his life because of Bodie and he wouldn't think of moving on until he had his face off with the man hunter. He knew all about Bodie and his reputation. It meant nothing to Billy Dancer. He was more than confident over his ability to take the man. Damn right Bodie was a tough *hombre*. Dancer was smarter. His speed with his gun unrivalled and with the undiminished confidence of youth Dancer would face down the man hunter and show him who was better.

The only drawback was the need to trail through the desert in order to get to Bodie. The trek was taking its toll on Dancer. He was still weak. He tried to conserve his energy though the discomfort brought on by the slow ride was doing little to help. Dancer had rested his left arm across his body, holding it firm. Even so every time his horse took a heavy step it caused fresh surges of pain in his shoulder. He needed a doctor but there wasn't one in fifty miles. Maybe further. And making a visit to any town would only add to the chances of Dancer being recognized. *Damned if he did — damned if he didn't.* Whichever course he took Billy Dancer was going to be faced with choices.

He unhooked his canteen, keeping

the reins in his right hand, and took a slow swallow of warm water. He swilled out his mouth and spat, then took a further drink to ease his parched throat. It made him think of Bodie. Dancer had shot a hole in his canteen back at the gully. By now Bodie would be suffering. His throat and mouth so dry it had to hurt. That allowed Dancer a small degree of satisfaction. Anything that might make the man hunter suffer was fine as far as Dancer was concerned.

Just don't let that suffering be too bad, he thought.

He didn't want Bodie expiring before they got to him. Bodie's death had to be up close and personal else it wouldn't have the same degree of satisfaction. It had to be personal.

'Horses need to rest,' Benedict said.

Cagle nodded and they reined in. Coming down off their saddles they loosened the saddle girths. Upturning their hats they poured in water and let the horses wet their muzzles. When he saw Dancer struggling one-handed Benedict helped him out and Dancer offered a grudging murmur of thanks.

It was a natural thing to look after the horses. No man with a lick of sense would force an animal to walk the desert without looking out for it. If he didn't and pushed his mount to the limit he might end up on foot himself. Men would curse and yell at their horses at times, but in rough country they treated them right — unless they were simple-minded to the point of recklessness.

When they had rested for a while they moved out, leading the horses for a half hour before taking to the saddles again.

'Still damned hot,' Dancer grumbled.

'Gets chilled at night sometimes,' Cagle said. 'Desert never seems to settle one way or the other.'

'We do for Bodie,' Benedict said, 'he won't need to worry about that.'

'He'll be burning in hell,' Dancer said. 'Make sure of that.'

11

Mid-afternoon and Bodie figured he had no more sweat to give. He was parched dry from head to foot. The overwhelming heat struck him like hammer blows and his body ached all over. His head pulsed with a monotonous regularity. He had turned up the collar of his shirt to protect the back of his neck but there was little else he could do to protect himself from the sun. He was out in the open, with nothing to offer shade and until he reached Pinto Wells there was no relief.

Bodie simply kept moving. He was single-minded once he set a course. In this instance he had little choice to do otherwise.

Three hostile guns at his back.

The unforgiving desert spread around him.

Pinto Wells ahead promising him the

only salvation he was about to be offered.

He narrowed his eyes against the sun's reflected glare. The pale sand threw the light back in his face and generated enough heat to be felt through the soles of his boots.

As hard as his situation was Bodie refused to let it get to him. There was no point. He was here. Had no way of escaping the moment, so he kept moving, letting his mind conjure up what it was going to be like when he reached the *tinajas*. That was something positive.

The smooth rock formations. The deep pans holding the cool, clear water that bubbled up through the fractured strata. Somewhere in the depths of his heat-frazzled mind he remembered the words that explained the phenomenon that allowed Pinto Wells to exist. *Artesian well*. That was it. Water beneath the ground being pushed to the surface through natural pressure. Bodie tried to recall where he had heard the phrase but it evaded him. His dry lips formed a thin smile. *Hell of a time to start remembering something like that*, he decided. Not that it was going to help much. The only thing that really mattered was actually reaching Pinto Wells so he could dunk his head in the water. Drink his fill. Wash away the gritty sand that was creeping into every part of him.

The only way to make that happen was to keep walking. One slow step at a time. He felt the thin stir of the desert wind. It lifted grains of sand that peppered his legs. Bodie lifted his head and studied the big sky, wondering if there was going to be another blow. The breeze remained slight. Just a faint disturbance that touched the surface of the desert. It didn't become any stronger. Nearby he heard the soft rustle of dried grass making sound as the wind disturbed it. A flicker of movement caught his eye and he spotted the rapid slide of a lizard as it skittered its way across the sand.

Despite its barren appearance there was life around him. Lizards. Snakes. Always something.

And right now the most dangerous form of life was crossing the desert.

Man.

The species that killed without thought. Killed because of anger. Greed. Or simply because it could.

Bodie's mind conjured up the image of his three pursuers.

Violent, vengeful men who were determined to make him pay for what he had done to them. In their minds Bodie was fair game. His actions had stripped them of their freedom. Condemned them to three years behind the bars of Yuma. The fact they had robbed and murdered to feed their greed made no difference in their eyes. Caught, sentenced for their crimes and imprisoned. Cagle, Benedict and Dancer had sweated out close on three years. With nothing to do but let their hate fester. To build until it became the one thing that kept them alive. Existing on the bile that gathered in their throats. The bitter anger that grew and became the single thing that kept them sane.

And now they were free they had decided to collect. To reach out with that savage need for pure, undiminished retribution.

For the man who had taken their freedom and had them locked away. It was driving them now. The force that had brought them to the desert wasteland in their search for Bodie.

★   ★   ★

'*Son of a bitch*,' Dancer yelled. 'I see him. Bodie. Out there.'

He yanked his Henry from its scabbard. Favoring his left arm he jacked a shell into the breech.

'Now,' he said. 'Now's the time. Before he gets to cover at the wells.'

'Ease off, Billy,' Cagle said. 'We've got him. Don't push it.'

Dancer's thin face was suffused with anger, his eyes wild with impatience.

'*The hell with waiting*,' he said. 'I want that mother. I want him now while he's in the open with nowhere to hide.'

'Billy, I said no.'

Dancer swung his rifle in Cagle's direction.

'You leave me be. Don't tell me what to do. You ain't my goddam father. He used to tell me what to do. He was a bully. Until the day I shot him down. Now stay off my back . . .'

Dancer stabbed his heels into his horse's side. It lunged forward, Dancer gripping its flanks with his thighs as he sped away from his partners.

'*Billy* . . .'

Benedict caught hold of Cagle's arm.

'Leave him be, Vince. That idiot boy is bound and determined to get himself killed. Ain't no use trying to stop him.'

'Bodie's liable to shoot him out the saddle.'

'And you and I can't do a damn thing to stop it.'

Bodie had halted on a slight rise, scanning the way ahead through red-rimmed and aching eyes. He used an arm to shield his gaze as he focused in on a shadowy outline on the near horizon, blinking to clear his vision. Through the shimmer of heat haze he traced the image. It lay to his right. Hard to determine just how far it was. The distorted imagery could fool a man into believing something was closer than it actually was and played tricks on him. He crouched and took his time as he studied the image.

Pinto Wells?

Or some imaginary object that might have been created by his fevered brain?

Bodie realized the only was he was going to find out was by heading straight for it.

Sitting here ain't going to bring it any closer, he said to himself. A croaky chuckle followed. *Talking to yourself now.*

He pushed to his feet, trying to ignore the stiffness invading his limbs, and walked on. Let himself conjure up an image of a deep, cool pool of water. That was what he was going to find when he reached Pinto Wells. Right now nothing else mattered to him. Not the desert. Not the three men trailing him. All that he wanted was to reach that water. Hear it splash as he scooped it up in his hands and sluiced it into his face. It became the image swimming before his eyes.

Precious water.

Cold and fresh and . . .

. . . he barely noticed the spurt of sand feet away as a bullet hit the ground.

But he did register the flat sound of the gunshot.

Bodie jerked into action, his right hand dropping to close around the butt of the heavy Colt. As he yanked it clear he turned and saw a horse and rider heading in his direction, the rifle held awkwardly because his left arm was stiff. The shooter jacked another round into the breech.

Bodie caught a glimpse of a wild face. Thin and bony. His hat had blown off, exposing the stringy hair streaming back. He didn't need a second look.

It was Billy Dancer.

He was screaming something as he spurred his horse on, directly at Bodie, the words lost as he fired a second time.

Sand slapped against Bodie's leg as the slug landed closer.

He closed his hand and palmed the Colt, using both hands as he brought it into play, ignoring the threat from Dancer's rifle.

The distance closed fast. A trail of dusty sand flew up from beneath the pounding hooves of Dancer's horse. Bodie held his position. Waited. Letting Dancer move well in range.

' . . . *of a bitch*,' were Billy Dancer's last words.

He angled his rifle in Bodie's direction, slow because of his wounded arm.

The big Colt slammed out its sound. Dancer's body jerked as the .45 slug took him in the left shoulder, close to where Bodie had shot him earlier. Dancer dropped his rifle, snatched at his holstered handgun, still yelling, and Bodie realized he wasn't about to give up.

Bodie saw the horse growing larger in his sight.

It was getting too close.

He pulled back on the trigger. Felt the revolver slap against his palm. His shot punched into Dancer. Bodie held the trigger back and emptied the Colt into him, working the hammer with his left hand. The slugs slammed into Dancer in one continuous roll of sound. Bloody flecks burst from Dancer's body. Two of the slugs exited through his spine, severing his ability to stay upright. Bodie pulled himself to the side as the spooked horse thundered by. Dancer toppled from the saddle and hit the ground in a loose sprawl.

Dancer's horse kept running, taking itself away from Bodie. He saw it go but made no attempt to chase after it. He had already spotted the distant shapes of Dancer's partners. They were still a ways off, holding back now while they waited to see what he was going to do. They were nowhere as impulsive as Dancer had been. Cagle and Benedict had a healthy respect for someone like Bodie. Seeing him take down Dancer would have cautioned them against making a foolish move — like the one that had got Dancer killed.

Bodie picked up the rifle Dancer had dropped. He checked the .44 caliber Henry repeater. It looked fine. Until he had the opportunity to check out the shots left he was going to have to hope Dancer had fully loaded it before he made his abortive charge. If it had a full magazine when Dancer rode after him, Bodie could have at least a dozen shots available. *If* it had been fully loaded.

If.

A small word that could make a hell of a difference.

Bodie spotted Dancer's handgun. It lay close to the bloody corpse. A .45 Colt's Peacemaker. It had all six chambers full. He tucked the revolver under his belt.

'Thanks for the loans, Billy,' he said. 'I'll make good use of them.'

He took a final look at Cagle and Benedict. They were still there. Well out of rifle range. Just watching. Unlike Dancer they were prepared to wait. Staying back while they dogged Bodie's trail. Right now they had the advantage.

They had horses.

They would have water.

And they had time to wait him out.

12

Silverbuck was riding in directly behind the men following Bodie. He kept his distance, using the contours of the land to conceal his presence. It wasn't difficult. The two whites were so intent on keeping Bodie in their sights they never once checked their back trail. Silverbuck was able to stop on a number of occasions an observe the scene ahead of him using his binoculars.

He saw the younger man break away from the older men and ride his horse wildly across the sand. Following his reckless charge, the equally reckless rifle fire, Silverbuck witnessed the brief challenge the young man threw down. There was an inevitability in the action as Bodie stood his ground and shot the man out of his saddle, took his weapons and moved on. The man hunter was still heading towards Pinto Wells.

The other men remained beyond rifle range, watching Bodie, and Silverbuck could imagine their thinking. They had seen how easily Bodie had dealt with the younger man and they were taking their time. The breed gave them credit for that. Even in their desire to reach Bodie and kill him, they were smart enough to understand the skill of their quarry. Not for them a swift, unthinking attack. They would watch and wait, picking their moment.

And Bodie would be doing the same. Letting them follow him. Allowing then to believe they could handle him in their own time.

Silverbuck smiled to himself, unconsciously rubbing at the rough scar on his neck.

I'm still here, Bodie. Getting closer you son of a bitch. Your time is coming.

★ ★ ★

'All the time we were in Yuma I had to listen to him moan and whine about how he was going to put Bodie down,' Benedict said. 'He was mistaken about most things. Seems he was wrong about that.'

'Tobe, you're all heart.'

Benedict leaned his hands on the saddle horn, focusing on Bodie's distant figure. He watched the man hunter collect Dancer's discarded weapons, then turn around and move off.

'Now we go chasin' him too close he'll pick us off with that Henry of Billy's like swattin' flies around a jam pot.'

'No arguing' that point. Appears we just stay out of range and allow for him to reach Pinto Wells. Then what?'

'Then we flank him. Come at him from two directions. Catch him in a crossfire. Even Bodie can't shoot at two targets at the same time.'

Cagle thought about that. 'It'll be dark in a couple hours. What if he slips away then?'

'Light or dark, Vince, he's still one man on foot. We're on horseback. Whichever way he'd go if he quits the wells we can ride him down if need be.'

'Let's hope you got this all worked out.'

'Christ, Vince, you're letting this get to you. I'll give you some news to cheer you up. When Bodie dealt with Elkins we were down to a three-way split.'

'So?'

'With Billy out of the count it's a two-way split now. Just you and me, partner.'

'Well, hell, I guess somebody had to point that out.'

'Crazy kid. Just couldn't bide his time.'

'That's the trouble with younkers. No sense of discipline.'

'Ain't that the livin' truth.'

They eased their horses into movement. Well behind the slow-moving figure of Bodie.

★ ★ ★

He reloaded his own Colt as he walked, then slid it back into the holster. Checking the Henry, Bodie took a look at the under-barrel follower. It was about a third of the way down the tube. He guessed he had at least ten .44-40 shots left out of the full magazine capacity. While he had the open magazine tube in his sights Bodie checked it for any sand that might have worked its way into the gap; the Henry was an excellent piece of weaponry, made with precision and workmanship, but the design of the magazine left it prone to becoming fouled up — the same applied to the open top frame; Bodie satisfied himself the weapon was clear. The last thing he needed was for the rifle to jam at a crucial moment.

Bodie had seen men die because their poorly maintained weapon jammed up on them during a gunfight. He never intended that to happen to him. He kept his own arsenal clean and in good working order. One of the drawbacks of using another man's guns was depending that he had been as keen on keeping them efficient as Bodie had become.

Even though the afternoon was drawing down, the temperature did not. Out on the open landscape of the desert there was nothing to ease the heat. It burned its way across the rolling expanse, sparing no one. There was no relief. No shade. Just the glare of the harsh light bouncing off the parched land.

Bodie had little concept of how long he'd been walking. It was simply a case of one foot before the other. Sloughing through the sand that drew his boots in and made each step an effort.

When he finally paused to check his progress he saw the dark outline of the rocks that made up Pinto Wells no more than a quarter mile ahead. He took a long look, mainly to convince himself he was really seeing the place. That it wasn't his eyes playing tricks on him. That he was not seeing a heat-created mirage. The thought he might be close brought a moment of elation. Then he turned and saw that the pair of riders behind him had increased their pace. They must have realized how near he was to the wells and were closing the distance.

Bodie worked his dry lips, trying to draw a little moisture from his mouth, but there was nothing to draw. He moved now, increasing his own pace. Dragging his heavy steps through the clinging sand. Fighting off the fatigue threatening to slow his efforts. The effort cost him. His dehydrating body was resisting his efforts.

'*No damn way*,' he said. '*You don't give up now.*'

He stumbled, going down on one knee.

Anger rose. He twisted around and brought the rifle to his shoulder, tracking the approaching riders, even though he was aware they had to be still beyond range. He fired off a pair of shots, the slam of sound from the Henry loud in the desert stillness. He didn't wait to see if the shots made any difference. Bodie pushed to his feet and kept moving. A single thought crossed his mind.

At least the damn rifle worked.

13

Bodie was as close to running as his weary, heat-soaked body would allow when he hit the outlying dark rocks that marked the beginning of Pinto Wells. He barely registered the sound as his boots touched the smooth curve of the eons-old formation. All he registered was the fact he had actually made it and the promise of water had become a reality. That was if the damned place hadn't dried up before he got there. He dismissed the errant thought. It was just his mind playing tricks on him.

He moved up the rising slope of rock, stepping to the higher level of the wells, searching, seeking the one thing he needed right then more than anything else.

As he stumbled his way across the rock surface he saw the gleam of water in front of him. The placid, inviting shine of the pools. He knew there were at least four of them. All fed by the precious water that pushed its way from deep underground and forced its way out through the fissures. The water tumbled from the highest point, bubbling lazily down over the smooth-worn stone to fill the main pan, which in turn spilled into the smaller hollows.

Bodie dropped to his knees by the closest pool. He scooped up water and splashed it on his dry face. The chill of the water against his heated flesh was a shock. He felt it against his rough lips. Swallowed some and it was the best-tasting water he had ever felt. The urge was there to drink until he was sated, but he held back. Too much was as dangerous as none at all. If he overfilled his stomach he could easily end up with cramps. He leaned over and took a couple of mouthfuls, allowing the water to trickle down his parched throat. Then he dunked his head under the surface, coming back up and shaking his head, water spraying wildly, scrubbing his free hand through his hair to loosen the dusty sand that had settled there.

As much as he wanted to relax Bodie knew he could not let that happen. Cagle and Benedict were still trailing after him, and now he had reached the comparative safety of Pinto Wells, they would be closing in. He scooped up a final drink, brushed his hair back from his face and turned to see what was happening.

Cagle and Benedict were moving in. With a difference now. They had split apart, each man coming from a separate direction. They were going to catch Bodie between them. Give him two targets to deal with. He watched their slow, deliberate approach. Still keeping out of range, making wide circular approaches. They were thinking this out. A sight smarter than Billy Dancer's head on charge.

Bodie backed off, seeking his best position. Pinto Wells was an island of rock set in the desert sand. A mass of weathered rocks that ranged from man-sized chunks up to boulders the size of a house. Some even larger. A seemingly haphazard collection that might have been assembled by a giant's hands. Here and there within the gaps and cracks were clumps of tough grass, cholla, ocotillo. Bodie saw ironwood and mesquite around the perimeter. Hardy plants that had gained a foothold and survived by drawing moisture that seeped into the soil as overspill from the rock pans. Bodie spotted a Gecko lizard sunning itself on a flat rock. He knew there would be rattlesnakes around too, most likely staying in the shade. As long as they were not disturbed Bodie didn't see them as a threat.

He stepped up on one of the highest boulders. It allowed him to see the surrounding area clearly. And pick out Cagle and Benedict.

Cagle was to the west, his partner more or less east. At that moment they were patiently sitting their saddles, watching. Bodie knew that situation was not going to last forever. The pair would make their move when it suited them and Bodie was going to have to face that when it happened.

14

Bodie felt the desert breeze stirring across Pinto Wells. It disturbed the brittle vegetation. Sent silver ripples across the pools of water. He heard the dry rattle of sand pattering against the stones. Felt it pluck at his shirt. The overbearing heat of the sun eased off as it began its descent in the west. Shadows lengthened.

It had been a hell of a day, Bodie decided, and the night wasn't promising to be much better.

He checked all his weapons again. Just to be sure. Both Colt pistols were fully loaded and he figured he had in the region of seven, eight shots left in the Henry. Plus the cartridges in his belt. He wasn't entirely short on ammunition, but to make good use he needed to be able to spot his targets. The closer it came to dark the less opportunity he was going to have.

Sooner or later he was going to have to make a decision. Wait for Cagle and Benedict to come looking for him — or take the fight to them. Neither solution offered much in the way of comfort. However Bodie approached the problem he knew one thing for certain. It was going to end in a burst of violence. The bitter fact was as solid as the inevitability of the sun going down.

★   ★   ★

Darkness followed as the sun dropped behind the western horizon. Heat came off the dry land, the temperature beginning to drop. It was a slow process, so gradual it was easy not to notice until the chill began to invade the body.

Silverbuck had already drawn a blanket around his shoulders. He had Pinto Wells in his sights. Able to see the pair of waiting *Pinda Lickoyi*. He was curious as to how they were going to strike against Bodie. The man hunter was at the high point of the island of rocks, most likely able to watch his enemies and left with the choice of which one to deal with first.

Bodie was skilled. He would make a decision and when he struck it would be quickly and Silverbuck had no doubt deadly. Bodie gave little quarter. He killed without hesitation when there was the need and he was the one who decided on that need.

Silverbuck watched. And waited. Knowing his time was coming. The time when he, who used to be called Massai, would take his revenge for his earlier defeat at the hand of the one called Bodie. It had been a long time and Silverbuck had asked *Ussen* on many occasions to grant him the power to find and defeat Bodie. Now that wish was to be allowed and Bodie *would* die.

As he observed Silverbuck allowed a smile to curl his mouth. Even thought the one called Bodie was an enemy, there was respect in Silverbuck. It was how it should be. There would be little honor in killing a man he did not respect. There was enough Apache blood in Silverbuck to have those thoughts for his opponent. And it would sit well that when he killed the *Pinda Lickoyi* it would be a deed well done.

★　★　★

Tobe Benedict shifted uncomfortably in his saddle. He was beginning to think this was not such a good idea after all. Dancer was dead and Cagle — well Cagle was bound and determined to have his reckoning with the bounty man.

Bodie was sitting somewhere in the mass of rocks most likely just waiting them out because there wasn't much else he could do. They had done what they set out to do. Get him at a disadvantage. But it even that wasn't working out exactly as planned.

Now they had shot his horse from

under him and pushed him into the desert, on foot, and with only his handgun. That was until *he* had shot and killed Dancer. Which had been the kid's own fault going off hog wild and not doing much thinking before he acted. Bodie had put him down. Had also taken Dancer's rifle and lit out to hide in the rocks of Pinto Wells.

Benedict still wanted his piece of flesh. No denying that. But he was starting to wonder if this was the way to do it. Bodie was lodged in the rocks while he and Cagle were standing watch over him. They were staying well out of rifle range. The trouble there was that it worked both ways. While Bodie's rifle couldn't reach them they couldn't get to him with theirs. It was a standoff. No argument. Benedict was hard put trying to figure out how they were going to break that stalemate.

Deciding he'd sat long enough Benedict slid out of the saddle to ease his aching bones. Thinking hard he started to come around to believing maybe they hadn't gone about this the best way they could. It had seemed a good idea at the start but after losing Elkins and his two men, and then Dancer, Benedict realized they had already paid a big price and still had Bodie to deal with. Benedict was ready to admit the man they were up against was one of the best. The man hunter worked in a direct, no-questions-asked manner. There was little sentiment in the way he operated. The man was relentless. He never quit once he was dogging a man's trail and it was a known fact he brought in more men dead than alive. It saved a lot of problems that way. Reduced the need for a trials and cut through the paperwork. Give the man a wanted poster and there was little more needed doing.

Benedict looped his reins around a tough stem of ocotillo, hoping the tether would persuade his horse to stay put. The animal was as weary as its rider, so Benedict was expecting it to remain where it was. He slid his Winchester into the scabbard and pulled out his Colt. The handgun would work better close up, because that was what Benedict was about to venture. He had run out of patience as far as waiting for Cagle to make a move.

With shadows deepening Benedict closed in on the mass of rocks, pausing often and telling himself this was a damn sight better than just sitting on his butt waiting — waiting for what? He still wasn't clear in his mind what his partner had in mind. Cagle had a habit of making decisions but not always passing those decisions on.

So this time Tobe Benedict was making the move himself.

It was his ass on the line so he figured he should make the choice.

He reached the outer barrier of Pinto Wells. Crouched against the rocks where he could still feel heat residue through his shirt. Apart from a whispered soughing of wind and the occasional rattle of drifting sand it was quiet. The near silence could be unnerving. The absence of extraneous noise was something that put Benedict's nerves on edge.

He debated the need for silence himself. If he was expecting to catch Bodie unaware he would sure as hell need to do it without a lot of noise.

Benedict sat down and eased off the boots. Leather soles and hard heels were not the quietest footwear. And the spurs he wore attached had a habit of jingling unexpectedly. His thick socks would muffle any movement he made. Benedict balanced his hat over the top of the boots when he stood them together.

Son, you've done some crazy things in your life but this one tops them all.

Then he eased around the fringe of Pinto Wells until he was able to start to climb. Benedict negotiated the first rocks, his eyes searching the shadows. They crisscrossed the rock faces, making it hard to separate actual images from imaginary.

Benedict figured Bodie would have chosen a high point that would give him a clear eye line. Which meant it was possible he might have seen Benedict's approach. He understood he could already be in the bounty man's sights. It was an unnerving thought. Too late to back away now.

Benedict was fully committed. And he had no thoughts on backing away. Whatever else Tobe Benedict might be he was no coward. Bodie was good, he gave the man that, but in the end he *was* only human. And that meant he could be killed as well as the next man.

As he moved Benedict allowed a single thought to fill his mind.

Three years.

Three years spent locked away in that stinking hole they called Yuma Pen. Years of his life take from him because of Bodie. Benedict's fingers gripped the butt of the Colt. Years he could never get back. So he was doing this to pay Bodie back. Benedict had lost three years — now Bodie was going to lose his life.

15

Bodie, never one to take anything at face value, had kept a constant watch on Cagle and Benedict's moves. It proved harder as the day's light began to fade. He found himself having to alternate between the pair, wishing one of them would move closer so he could use the Henry rifle. They didn't, so his hope was left dangling. It was obvious the two were playing a waiting game. There was not going to be a wild attack similar to the one that had brought Billy Dancer down. Cagle and Benedict were old hands. Men who had lived too long to throw their lives away on a whim. They were content to sit and wait until the moment came.

The sun was well below the horizon and Bodie felt something was going to happen any time soon. He wasn't far off with his guessing. He had been watching the waiting riders, shifting his gaze back and forth because it was all he could do. Cagle and Benedict separating had put pressure on Bodie. He had no choice but to keep checking between the pair. Shifting position to keep them each in sight.

And then he saw that Benedict had gone from his saddle. In the time Bodie had been watching Cagle, Tobe Benedict had moved. His riderless horse stood motionless and Bodie knew that Benedict was moving in towards Pinto Wells.

It had happened, he had missed it, and there was no point in berating himself. Bodie eased his way across the rocks, checking the open ground between Benedict's former position and the beginning of the wells. He had to give Benedict marks for a fast move. If the man kept to his first move he was about to stay quiet. Climb up from ground level and tackle Bodie head on.

Bodie laid the Henry down. A rifle was ideal for long distance shooting but could be unwieldy up close. A hand-gun, or even a knife would be better for the kind of killing Benedict would have in mind. He was making this personal. There would be a great deal of feeling behind Benedict's move.

Three years of feeling. Anger that would have built up while the man was behind Yuma's stone walls and iron bars.

Bodie crouched in the shadows, his senses tuned to pick up any sign of Benedict's approach.

Time went by unnoticed. The shadows around Bodie lessened slightly as starlight cast a soft glow over Pinto Wells. It was not direct light but dissipated the darkness slightly and gave Bodie the chance to observe anything that moved within his vicinity.

Bodie had developed the ability to remain still for long periods. A trait that his profession demanded. It came from his need to watch and wait for his man to move closer. To hold back until the time was right, because that difference was the measure between life and death. Over the years Bodie had developed his skill from not just practice, but by observing others. He had taken his cue studying them. Indian and white had been his teachers and Bodie had absorbed what he saw. Stilling his body, slowing his breathing, training his eyes to pick up the slightest of movements. To see and hear the minutest suggestions that betrayed the presence of another human. He took it all in when the chance arose until it had become part of himself.

He saw a flicker of movement in the shadows of a rock outcrop. The faintest shift of darkness that detached from the deeper whole. There had been no reason for the occurrence. So it meant the presence of something — more likely *someone*. Too high off the level to have been caused by a small creature like a lizard. The bulk suggested a human animal flitting silently by.

Tobe Benedict most likely.

Bodie gave the man his due. He had

breached the rock formation with ease. Silent and fast.

Bodie remained still. His attention focussed on the spot. Now he could make out the crouched form of the man, Benedict's shape slowly coming into view as he cleared the bulk of rock and exposed himself. Faint light slid along the metal of the gun in Benedict's right hand.

Bodie eased his left hand back to the knife sheathed on his side. He drew the keen blade and passed it to his right hand. He hadn't wanted to pull his Colt. Even easing back the hammer might cast a faint sound that could reach Benedict's ears. The knife was silent, in operation and delivery.

Close now, no more than a few feet, Benedict froze, the dark shape of his head casting from side to side. He was checking his position, searching for Bodie. Caution dictating his actions. He rose from his lowered position and it seemed to Bodie the man had reached a decision.

When Benedict moved his gun hand round Bodie pushed forward, coming out of his dark corner and struck with frightening speed, left hand reaching to grip the man's gun wrist, the cold blade of his knife streaking in at Benedict's body. The blade sank in to the hilt, Bodie twisting it hard.

Benedict let out a high, shivering scream of pure terror as he felt the blade cutting into his body.

His finger jerked on the trigger and his gun slammed out a shot.

Bodie worked the knife in the wound, ignoring Benedict's agonised screams. He wanted the matter over and done. He felt the warm spurt of blood from Benedict's body. Sliding his hand along Benedict's wrist Bodie grabbed for the pistol and wrenched it free. He heard it clatter against rock when he dropped it. Benedict struck out with his fists, catching Bodie alongside the head, but his blows were already weakening. Bodie reached up and clamped his free hand around

Benedict's throat, fingers digging in. He pushed Benedict back a few steps until the man came up against a slab of rock. Bodie held him there as Benedict struggled against the encroaching weakness his massive blood loss had caused.

' . . . wanted you dead,' he said, his voice gone to a soft whisper, the effort almost too much.

'Not happening,' Bodie said. 'You first . . . '

He gave the knife a final thrust and Benedict's legs slid from under him. Bodie let the man go, Benedict slumping to the surface of the rock, loose and looking like a man without bones.

Bodie stepped back, the bloody knife hanging at his side. He was sweating despite the chill in the air. Then he turned and stared off to where he had seen Vince Cagle sitting his horse.

Cagle was on the move, his mount picking its way in the direction of the wells.

'Come get some,' Bodie said softly and walked to where he had laid down his rifle.

He slid the bloody knife back in its sheath, checked the Henry and his holstered Colt.

He wanted this to be over. Done. And the hell with bringing in Cagle alive to tell where he had hidden all that stolen gold. As far as Bodie was concerned Cagle was just another wanted man, with a reward posted for him. If he did bring in Cagle dead he wasn't going to be popular with the banks that had lost money. The hell with them, Bodie decided, he wasn't in business to try and win friends. He simply wanted to stay alive.

16

Bodie eased to the edge of the rocks and watched Vince Cagle ride down from where he'd been waiting. A full moon was rising, casting a cold light that let Bodie follow Cagle's progress as he brought himself into range. The move was deliberate. As if Cagle no longer worried over presenting himself as an open target. He must have heard Benedict's single gunshot.

He couldn't have known it came from Benedict's gun. It might have easily been Bodie's shot. Either way Cagle was taking a big risk. He knew Bodie's reputation. Would have understood he was putting himself in a position where Bodie could take a clear shot.

Bodie shouldered the Henry, easing his finger to the trigger and put Cagle in his sights.

Then Cagle's left arm swept up, the rifle he was holding snapping into position and he began to trigger a burst of shots aimed at Bodie's position. The shots were close, tearing off splinters of rock and flinging them at Bodie. He drew back, feeling the sharp sting across the side of his face and by the time he searched for Cagle the man had disappeared in the dark overhang of the rock mass.

He had to give credit to Cagle. The man had worked fast, not expecting his volley to find a definite target, but heavy enough to make Bodie pull back.

Bodie turned and crossed the high rocks, using what light from the moon he could to show him where Cagle might be. When he paused, listening, he picked up the sound of boots scraping against rock. It made him think back to something that had barely registered at the time. The sight of Benedict's stockinged feet as he had fallen in front of Bodie. A simple enough thing to do — remove his boots to muffle the sound of his approach.

Not something Vince Cagle had thought about. He might have reached Bodie's refuge, but he was advertising his presence in his hurry to get to the man hunter.

'Bodie. You son of a bitch, I'm on my way. You figure to take me down like you done for Dancer and Benedict. I'm guessing you took Tobe. Yeah? Well not Vince Cagle, you miserable son. I aim to blow holes in you big enough to show daylight. Then I'll go pick up my gold and live high on the hog.'

Bodie heard the words and heard the rattle and scrape of Cagle as he stepped up the rocks of Pinto Wells.

He didn't respond. Simply waited for Cagle to show himself. The man had worked himself into a frenzy that was making him lax. He was ignoring his own earlier caution in his eagerness to get to the man he held responsible for his life's downturn.

Bodie waited, letting Cagle come to him, and did nothing to dissuade him.

He had no problem with allowing the other man to put himself willingly on the road to hell.

Cagle reared into view on the level just below where Bodie stood. He stepped into the open, swinging his rifle back and forth as he looked for his target. Bodie saw him as a gray silhouette. A moving shadow. Only the metallic gleam of the rifle he carried showing clearly.

'*Bodie*. Show yourself . . . '

'I'm here,' Bodie said and put a shot into Cagle's side that pitched him forward. He let go of his rifle and it hit the rock and slid out of reach.

Bodie's slug had cored in deep and Cagle pulled himself upright and turned to face Bodie. His right hand pressed to the bloody wound in his side.

'*Oh, you bastard*. That was a sneaky shot.'

'You expect good manners? One question, Cagle, you going to tell me where the gold is?'

'What do you think, bounty man?'

There was the start of a grin on Cagle's lips as he went for his holstered Colt. Confidence in his eyes because he still believed he was fast enough to buck Bodie's rifle. His fingers had barely touched the butt when Bodie shot him, planting three more .44-40 lead slugs in him. Cagle uttered a stunned cry. He went back and stepped over the edge of the rock slope. His cry trailed off as he fell into the darkness, hitting the rocks below with a dull sound.

'Now that's got to be messy,' Bodie said softly. 'Be hell to wrap in a blanket.'

17

From his place beyond Pinto Wells Silverbuck had watched the *Pinda Lickoyi* called Bodie as he made ready his preparations to leave. After his kills he had brought together the horses his enemies had used and secured them. Before he rested he watered the animals, making sure they were settled before he took to his blanket and slept. It would have been easy then for Silverbuck to have reached the wells and killed Bodie while he did so. But that would have been too simple. And striking in the dark brought its own problems. Silverbuck stayed where he was, waiting for the dawn, so that the *Pinda Lickoyi* could see the face of his enemy when death found him.

Silverbuck had his horse at his side, the reins looped around one ankle to warn him if the animal tried to wander, or was startled by something disturbing the quiet. He also kept his rifle in his hands, laid across the body, the weapon loaded and ready.

First light touched his face and Silverbuck woke easily, shrugging his blanket from his shoulders as he eased himself into the day, stretching his cramped muscles. The arm Bodie had broken ached as it always did in the mornings so he flexed it until the nagging went away. He drank from his canteen, clearing his mouth, then offered water to his horse by filling a shallow rawhide dish from the pack on its back. He chewed on a strip of dry meat as he watched Bodie emerge from his own blanket and refresh himself in the cold water of the main *tinaja* of Pinto Wells. Silverbuck knew the deep tanks of the wells. Had tasted the fresh water that sprang from beneath the dark rocks himself. He saw the man hunter kneel and thrust his head beneath the surface, emerging to sluice his face and brush back his dark hair.

Silverbuck crouched and watched Bodie strip the saddle and gear from one of the tethered horses. He wrapped the bodies of the dead men in blankets, securing them with lengths of rope cut from one of the saddle ropes. Then he hoisted each body over the back of the stripped horse and tied them in place. The horse fidgeted when the bodies were first draped in place but Bodie spoke to it, soothing it and the animal settled down. Bodie drained both canteens he took from the horses and filled them with fresh water from the main tank. Even though he had most likely seen to the weapons he had gained, Bodie checked them all again. Satisfied he took the time to insect each horse, making sure they were ready for travel. Only then did he swing into the saddle of the horse he had chosen to ride and moved off, leading the second horse close behind.

Once Bodie had cleared Pinto Wells Silverbuck moved himself. He had no need to hurry. Bodie would be moving at a steady pace, letting his horse pick its own pace as the heat of the new day increased. Silverbuck could find the man easily in the open desert.

He rode down to Pinto Wells. Dismounted and led his horse to the welcome coolness of the *tinajas* where he let the animal drink. Silverbuck refreshed himself, then refilled his canteen with fresh water. He fed the horse with some of the grain he carried in a sack hung from his gear. Ate some dried meat himself.

Only when he was satisfied did he move on from the wells, easily able to spot the trail Bodie had left behind.

As Silverbuck rode on Pinto Wells was left empty and silent once again. Soon the desert breeze would drift the sand and cover the tracks and it would be as if no one had visited the place.

★ ★ ★

As Bodie took his leave from Pinto Wells the only thought on his mind was one of relief. He had walked into the place knowing there were two men on his trail with little on *their* minds except pure killing. Which was nothing new given Bodie's line of work. He took that as expected.

He felt the first rays of the sun and tugged down the brim of the hat he'd found at the base of the rocks where Tobe Benedict had left it with his boots before his climb up onto Pinto Wells.

On his return towards Yuma he found he was retracing his earlier trail though the tracks left from that journey had gone, wiped away by the windstorm of the previous day and the ever-present sloughing of the desert breeze. The feel of the hot sun, with the temperature rising quickly, forced him to ride slowly. Thought he had water now he still felt the after effects of his long walk. His lips were still dry, sore from the effects of his long trek and his face still showed the effects of the forced exposure. If he hadn't known the location of Pinto Wells and eventually reached the water, matters might have been resolved differently.

When he reached the general area where he had confronted Billy Dancer he checked around but couldn't find any sign. Not that he had expected to. Dancer was still in the desert but he was hidden from view now. Drifting sand, ever on the move could have sifted over the body. Sometime in the future, moving wind would expose his bones and maybe someone would find them and wonder who the dead man was. Not today. Not now, and Bodie had little interest in the dead. Only the living concerned him.

Right then he was the only one who mattered. The only one on the desert.

So he thought.

18

Silverbuck rode his own trail. Close enough to keep Bodie in sight, yet able to remain unseen by using the desert terrain to provide cover. Hollows and ridges in the landscape allowed the breed to follow Bodie without himself being spotted. The rising heat of the day had little effect on him. Desert such as this was home to Silverbuck. He could see from the way Bodie rode, hunched over in his saddle, that the heat was affecting him. The *Pinda Lickoyi* was no beginner. He knew the harsh ways of the land and treated it accordingly. Had he not survived on foot, walking across the desert to reach the sanctuary of Pinto Wells? And had then defeated the two men who had forced him into the desert. It took a special kind of man to take on such odds and survive — especially for a *Pinda Lickoyi*.

Urging his horse across a stretch of terrain where scrubby brush and scattered rocks lay, Silverbuck pulled back on his reins to walk around the area. It was in places like this that lizards and snakes hid themselves away from the harsh rays of the sun, choosing the cooler shadows on the vegetation. The breed's momentary lapse had allowed his horse to step close to the fringes of the brush, its head lowering as its curiosity caused it to investigate the movement with the brush. The warning rattle came too late and though Silverbuck hauled the horse's head around, there was little time to move his mount into the clear. Silverbuck caught a glimpse of the mottled skin. The sudden rapid movement of the rattlesnake, disturbed and hostile. It rose, extending its long body. The large head lunged forward, so fast it was a blur. It struck once, then again, sinking its curved fangs into the horse's muzzle and injecting the glistening venom. The panicked horse reared back, uttering a frightened sound and Silverbuck was forced to haul in on the reins, gripping with his legs in an attempt to keep the horse under control. The animal's exertions only succeeded in pushing the snake's injected venom deeper into its system. Silverbuck felt it bucking and writhing beneath him. The horse was fully out of control now, kicking and rearing. Silverbuck knew what was going to happen and he cleared the saddle, snatching his rifle from the scabbard as he jumped aside. He saw the horse go down, its bulk landing hard. It lay on its side, flanks quivering, eyes rolling with fear as it struggled to breathe through rapidly swelling airways. The snake slithered away and Silverbuck watched it go with a disinterested eye. The snake had only been acting the way it was supposed to. It had sensed a threat, real or not, and had reacted instinctively.

Silverbuck turned and made his way

to the top of the ridge. He bellied down and peered across the sand. Bodie was not moving. He was sitting his saddle, checking around him, listening, and Silverbuck knew the man hunter had heard enough to alert him.

This was not what Silverbuck had been expecting. He had wanted to be able to reach Bodie before the *Pinda Lickoyi* was aware. Now he would be on guard more than normally. Which would make Silverbuck's strike harder.

Behind him Silverbuck could hear the injured horse grunting, the sound growing more pronounced as the animal succumbed to the increasing restrictions of suffocation. The more it struggled the worse it became, the venom coursing through its system. He slid his heavy knife from its sheath and strode around the thrashing horse. With expert strokes he cut into the animal's neck, severing the main arteries. Hot blood flushed from the deep cuts and soaked into the parched ground and the horse's struggles quieted down as it died.

Silverbuck returned to observe Bodie. The *Pinda Lickoyi* was still there. Dismounted now and with his rifle in his hands as he looked about him.

Crouched behind the ridge, the desert breeze drifting the sand in lazy swirls, Silverbuck studied his enemy.

'I'm here, Stalker,' Silverbuck said. 'You look long enough and you *will* see me.'

His voice came out as a harsh whisper, almost a hiss of sound that matched the gritty noise made by the dry sand in the desert wind.

Silverbuck still held his knife, the blade wet with the blood of the dead horse. He thrust it into the sand to clean it, turning it back and forth.

'The next blood on my blade will be yours, *Pinda Lickoyi*. And when I cut *your* throat I will not fail to kill you.'

19

'That was no drifting sand,' Bodie murmured. 'Or a heavy-footed lizard.'

He reined in his horse, the one Cagle had been riding, and took a long, slow look around. The ever-present wind drift made it difficult to pinpoint the sound but Bodie had a feeling it had come from beyond the rim of the sloping sand hill that ran parallel to his line of travel. That lay on his left. To his right the desert landscape was pretty level. There definitely was nothing to see out there.

Cagle's bunch were all dead, so he wasn't expecting any more hard cases to come barrelling over the rise. Bodie took off his hat and ran his sleeve across his brow, feeling the sweat that had formed. He snugged the hat back in place and took another slow look around. He wondered if maybe there were some of the Indian trackers in the area, still on the lookout for the escapees from Yuma. They hadn't shown their faces up to now and something told him they wouldn't be showing up. The prison warden had put out the order that Bodie was looking for Cagle and company and he wasn't to be interfered with, so the trackers had concentrated on the surviving pair from the work party who were still at large. There hadn't been any sign of them around the desert area. Knowing the trackers Bodie figured they would be staying in the country west and north where the terrain would be somewhat more hospitable for all concerned.

So that left Bodie wondering who else might be around. He didn't discount the possibility it might be hostile Apaches. Thought the general threat from renegades was greatly reduced now, with the numbers getting smaller, there were still some around. Fiercely against giving in to the greater number of *Pinda Lickoyi*, the defiant ones waged their war, resisting to the end. Scattered, dispossessed, they fought on. Hit and run strikes to steal and kill. They resorted to vicious murder raids, taking lives and possessions, then scattered into the desert lands and the mountains of Mexico. Like flitting shadows the Apaches risked all against the army, the lure of battle against their enemy, ignoring the superior numbers. For some death in battle, hopefully swift, was a better choice than submitting to captivity. A life of deprivation on some reservation was looked on as a slow way to die. Stripped of their homeland and made to exist on the whims of their overseers was something many Apaches had no time for. So they remained free to choose their own destiny. Yet in the end even the most determined were forced to surrender. That or die under the guns of the *Pinda Lickoyi*. For some it became the only way they could stay free.

The thought was in Bodie's mind as

he eased from the saddle, rifle in his hands, and took a long look around. He concentrated on the ridge, still with the feeling the sound he had heard was more than imaginary.

He began to be aware of the feeling he was being watched. Yet it was no more than a feeling. Maybe imagined because of where he was. The desert tended to create those sensations. Maybe nothing more than the mind playing tricks. Conjured up by the environment. The heat. The desert wind making its own voice heard. His own overriding weariness. Bodie moved around, still not sure what, if anything, he had heard — or imagined he had heard.

Behind him the horses stirred restlessly. Bodie moved back, took a drink from one of the canteens. He felt eyes on him. The horses were watching him drink. They managed to make him feel guilty, so he tipped water into his hat and let each animal drink.

'Just go easy,' he said. 'Since we left

the wells behind, there ain't no more for a distance.'

The horses pushed against him, wanting more, but he ignored them.

'Cut that out,' he told them. 'You get more when I decide when.' He rehung the canteen, shaking his head. 'Got me apologising to the horses now. I've been on this damned desert too long.

Bodie put the rifle away, took a final look around and mounted up. He took hold of the reins of the horse carrying the bodies and moved off. Still not fully satisfied, but accepting there wasn't much to be gained chasing after a sound that could have been nothing more than the wind stirring the sand and brush. If it had been anything more, charging up that rise he might have walked into a waiting gun. He had made his choice and he would have to live with it.

Or die from a bullet in the back.

For some reason that made him smile. He had no idea why. Maybe it was the way things had been happening over the last few days. Not exactly how he would have chosen, but up to now he had managed to stay alive and on his own two feet.

* * *

Silverbuck moved at a steady lope, far enough behind Bodie not to be seen, yet still able to track the man. He maintained his cover. Having seen the way Bodie acted Silverbuck knew the man was suspicious. Not enough to make him nervous, but a strong enough feeling to cause him to increase his wariness.

The breed moved easily, unhampered by the few possessions he carried. His weapons and ammunition pouch and the canteen he had freed from his horse. It was enough. For a man of Apache blood it was more than enough.

What else did he need in order to kill Bodie?

Even as he tracked the lone *Pinda Lickoyi* his warrior's mind was thinking ahead. To the moment when he finally confronted Bodie. He had realised that he wanted not only to have a face-to-face with Bodie, but he wanted — needed — to kill him with the cold steel of his knife. With the same type of weapon Bodie had tried to kill him with. Silverbuck would put aside his pistol and even his cut-down rifle. When he ended Bodie's life it would be with the naked steel of Silverbuck's razor edged knife. Killing Bodie that way would be justified in Silverbuck's mind. He wanted the man to feel the blade severing the flesh of his throat, spilling his blood the way Silverbuck's blood had run from his own throat. Only this time there would be no mistake. Bodie would die with his flesh cut open, staring into Silverbuck's eyes.

Bodie had his time coming. It would be Silverbuck's victory. He would see the *Pinda Lickoyi* die and leave his body to the *Zopilote*. When the vultures had done feeding on his flesh, Bodie's bones would be left to bleach under the desert sun.

20

Close on midday. The sun at its height. The heat getting to be overpowering. Even the sand underfoot was becoming hot. The ever-present desert breeze added to the stifling heat. Movement increased the effect and from his position on a sweeping curve of a sand hill Silverbuck saw the sluggish way Bodie leaned in his saddle. This was the time. When the man was at his lowest point.

Time for the kill.

Silverbuck was moving level with Bodie. Above him. Out of sight. He stripped off his shirt, took a final drink from his canteen. Then he laid the canteen on the sand, his rifle following and then his ammunition pouch. Now he had only his holstered Colt and his sheathed knife.

He allowed the slow-moving horse to

get a few feet ahead. Took steps back from the rim of the slope before launching himself forward, powering into a run.

Silverbuck reached the crest of the slope and hurled himself bodily into empty space, his leap taking him clear and then down at the rider.

Bodie heard the rush of movement. It came from his left and above him. He twisted in the saddle, eyes searching, and saw the blur of someone sweeping down on him from the top of the slope.

He had no chance to avoid Silverbuck as the breed came at him. Their bodies collided, Silverbuck slamming into Bodie's back, the impact driving him from the saddle. The two men cleared the horse, twisting in a tangle as they hit the ground, rolling and breaking apart, each pulling himself to his feet.

Bodie's rifle slid from his grasp as he landed.

They faced off, six feet apart, spitting out the sand that had got in their mouths. Ignoring the bruising aches resulting from the hard fall.

Bodie saw the dark-featured face. The scars and the deformities that marked it. The glittering eyes blazing with barely contained fury. And he saw the ridged scar that crossed the exposed throat.

It took him seconds to realize who he was facing.

The man he had left for dead.

Alive and ready to kill.

Silverbuck.

He pushed aside the fleeting sensation of surprise. Even shock because up until that moment he had never thought about the man since that day . . .

★ ★ ★

. . . Before Silverbuck could bring the knife back for a second cut Bodie, remembering he was still holding his Winchester, jabbed the hard butt of the stock against the side of Silverbuck's

face. Silverbuck grunted as the cheek bone cracked. Soft flesh split and blood welled from the ragged gash. Aware of the deadly knife the breed still held Bodie tossed his rifle aside and caught hold of Silverbuck's wrist, forcing the glittering blade away from his body. He shoved the heel of his right hand hard up against the underside of Silverbuck's jaw, pushing the breed's head back. There was a moment of panic and then Silverbuck regained control of his emotions. His left fist hammered down across Bodie's face. Bodie's head rocked to one side, pain flaring in his jaw. Blood streamed from a torn lip. He released his pressure on Silverbuck's jaw, drew his fist back, then clubbed the breed across the mouth. Silverbuck's face twisted in a rictus of agony. He spat blood and broken teeth. Bodie hit him again, crushing Silverbuck's nose. Blood squirted out in streams. Silverbuck wrenched himself away from Bodie, breaking the grip the man hunter had on his wrist. Letting

178

himself roll Silverbuck came to his feet swiftly, thrusting the knife out before him, point uppermost. Yet before he even saw his adversary, Bodie was on him. He had come to his feet as the breed had rolled away. The toe of his boot lashed up and out, catching Silverbuck in the stomach. White-hot pain speared his body. He stumbled back fighting for breath, tears stinging his eyes as he tried to see Bodie. But there was no chance to see Bodie. The man hunter stepped in close, grasping Silverbuck's knife wrist with one hand. Bodie's other arm slid beneath Silverbuck's limb, just above the elbow joint. Bodie put on the pressure, using Silverbuck's own weight as a lever. He thrust down hard against the arm joint, heard Silverbuck gasp, and thrust again. The arm bone snapped with an audible crack, the bone piercing the flesh of the arm, blood spurting from the wound. Silverbuck gave a low groan and slumped to his knees, the knife slipping forgotten from his hand.

Crouching, Bodie picked up the knife. He took hold of a handful of Silverbuck's black hair and yanked the breed's head back, pressing the tip of the knife against the taut throat.

'Now listen to me, you half-breed son of a bitch.' Bodie pressed on the knife so that the tip penetrated the flesh, letting a thin runnel of blood run down the breed's throat and across his naked chest. 'Don't play games with me. All I want from you is the name of the bastard who set you on my trail. Start remembering fast, 'cause you ain't got much time left.'

Silverbuck tried to twist his body away from Bodie. All that happened was that the blade of the knife sliced into his throat. Just deep enough to make the blood flow steadily.

'You keep wrigglin' about like that and you'll end up cutting your own throat,' Bodie said coldly. 'That would disappoint me somethin' awful, Silverbuck, 'cause I want to do the cuttin' myself.'

'Go to hell, you bastard,' Silverbuck hissed through clenched teeth. Sweat gleamed on his set, bronze face. He stared up at Bodie through eyes burning with hatred. 'I don't tell you a thing.'

Bodie slammed his right knee up into Silverbuck's face. He heard something crunch and as Silverbuck sagged back, blood gushed from his mouth. Silverbuck's head dropped against his chest. Blood streamed down his naked torso, soaking his pants. Still angry, Bodie hit the breed again, his fist coming down like a club. The blow struck Silverbuck across the back of his neck and he flopped face down on the ground, jerking softly, like a landed fish. Bodie planted brutal knee in Silverbuck's back, took hold of his hair again and yanked the breed's head up off the ground. Dirt had ground itself into the open gashes, clung to the sticky blood. He hardly seemed aware of his surroundings. Bodie pressed the keen edge of the knife against the rigid line of his throat.

'Who hired you, Silverbuck?'

Silverbuck spat blood. He began to dribble pink froth. 'Fuck, you, Bodie. You wan' kill me? Then go 'head.'

Bodie rammed his knee down hard. He heard Silverbuck's ribs crack. A low groan bubbled past the breed's lips. 'He must be payin' you a lot, Silverbuck. You figure it's worth it?'

'I ain't tellin' you a damn thing, Bodie.

Silverbuck's voice rose to a shrill protest, and it didn't stop until the blade of the knife in Bodie's sliced its way across his throat, laying it open. Silverbuck kicked and jerked for a time. Only when he was still did Bodie let the breed's head drop.

He stood up, still holding the knife and gazed down at the bloody corpse. Turning away to pick up his rifle Bodie murmured, 'Silverbuck, it seems like I've gone and cashed you in . . . '

* * *

. . . 'I see you remember me, Bodie. Silverbuck. No ghost, *Pinda Lickoyi*.'

The words from Silverbuck's lips sounded coarse, a raspy sound just above a whisper. A whisper maybe, but still filled with the hate the breed carried for the man who had inflicted the injuries on Silverbuck.

'Seems you're hard man to kill,' Bodie said.

He saw the Colt in Silverbuck's hand, aimed at him.

'Your gun. Throw it away,' Silverbuck said. 'We finish this the Apache way. If you have the courage.'

Bodie eased his Colt from the holster and cast it aside.

Silverbuck did the same, then produced the thick-bladed knife he carried.

Bodie pulled his own blade and held it so Silverbuck could see it clearly.

'You remember this?' Bodie said. 'I took it away from you last time we met. You want it back? Come and take it.'

Silverbuck weaved a pattern with his own blade, taking a stance that indicated he was ready to fight, and they circled each other. Each of them watching and waiting for an opening, eyes searching for any sign the other was about to strike.

Bodie's horses had wandered away from the area. Unconcerned. Overhead the sun made its daily journey and around them the desert made its soft sound as the wind blew across the sand.

Silverbuck lunged, the cold steel blade arcing in at Bodie's body. Bodie pulled back, but not quite fast enough and the edge of Silverbuck's knife cut through his shirt and sliced across his torso. The cut was not deep but it stung and Bodie gasped. A flicker of pleasure shone in Silverbuck's eyes.

First blood.

21

Bodie could feel blood streaming down his body. Soaking through his shirt. He pulled back, beyond Silverbuck's reach, never taking his eyes off the man. The breed had a faint smile edging his lips. He leaned in towards Bodie, arms spread, the fingers of his left hand moving as he flexed it. His knife made a feint at Bodie. The man hunter ignored it. Silverbuck was attempting to get a reaction. So Bodie refused to be taunted.

What he did instead was concentrate on Silverbuck's eyes. Waiting for the breed to signal his next move. He made an involuntary check before he struck, his eyes sliding to the left in the instant before he did strike.

Bodie was ready the next time he saw the warning and counter struck, weaving his body to one side and slashing with his own weapon. His blade cut across Silverbuck's left forearm. Opening an inches long gash that went in deep. Blood swelled up from the wound, running free and dripping from the limb. Bodie kept up his attack, knife arcing left and right, cutting, slashing, opening a number of gashes that drove Silverbuck back a few feet.

A ragged cry came from Silverbuck's lips, still low and hoarse. He dug in his heels and stood his ground, using his own weapon to hit back at Bodie. The steel of their blades clashed as they stood their ground, neither man willing to concede an inch. Sunlight glanced off the knives as they cut and slashed at each other. Blades found flesh and blood flew from the naked steel.

And then they were locked, each knife snagged at the hilt. Legs braced and feet digging in to prevent being pushed off balance.

Silverbuck slammed his bunched left fist into Bodie's face, feeling it split flesh. Bodie countered with a hard fist to Silverbuck's ribs, drawing a ragged gasp from the breed.

The stalemate maintained, they hammered at each other, each man attempting to break the knife hold. They were matched in strength and stubbornness. Muscles straining. Sweat gleamed on their faces. Bodie felt it mingling with the blood running down his own cheek, stinging wildly.

Bodie changed his stance without warning, stepping in closer to Silverbuck and looping his free arm around Silverbuck's neck. He kicked out with a booted foot, the heel cracking against Silverbuck's ankle. The hard blow was enough to lift Silverbuck's foot off the ground, leaving him briefly off balance. Still holding the breed close Bodie lifted and twisted. Silverbuck was spun to one side and Bodie kept up the momentum, turning Silverbuck in the air. The breed was lifted clear off the ground, but arched his body with a powerful turn and landed on his knees.

Bodie followed through and as

Silverbuck faced away from him he cut down at the breed's exposed back, the knife opening twin slashes in Silverbuck's flesh. Silverbuck grunted, falling forward and rolling clear before Bodie could strike again. He crabbed aside, on hands and knees, knowing Bodie would seek to maintain his attack, and as the man hunter drove in again Silverbuck stabbed upwards with his blade. It cut into Bodie's left thigh, sinking in a few inches, blood bursting from the severed flesh.

Ignoring the pain from the deep cuts in his back Silverbuck gained his feet, turning quickly to face Bodie and thrust himself forward as the *Pinda Lickoyi* bent forward, blood pouring from the wound in his leg.

A surge of hope rose in Silverbuck as he saw his enemy founder and he straightened his spine, unmindful of the hot blood streaming down his back.

He saw his victory so close now. Bodie weakened by the bleeding wounds in his body. Silverbuck stepped forward, reaching out to take hold on Bodie's hair.

And that was when Bodie brought his blade up from his waist, sinking it into Silverbuck's stomach. The force of the blow buried it to the hilt, cutting through flesh and muscle, deep into the breed's body. Silverbuck felt the shock of the blow, the surge of white-hot agony that coursed through him.

Bodie sawed the knife back and forth, opening the torso and spilling Silverbuck's entrails in a wet surge. As Silverbuck sank to his knees, dropping his own knife and clutching his body to stop his disembowelment, Bodie stepped close, then snagged Silverbuck's hair with his left hand and pulled the breed's head back. He raised the bloody knife and when he cut Silverbuck's throat this time he only stopped short of decapitating him.

He stood over the breed's shuddering body and didn't move until he was sure Silverbuck was really dead.

'If I had a goddam wooden stake I'd put it through your heart,' he said. 'Just to make sure you don't come back for a third time.'

Bodie looked down at the knife dangling from his bloody right hand. He wiped it against his shirt and pushed it into the sheath. He bent to pick up his Colt. The effort was too much and he dropped to his knees. Braced on his hands he let his head hang. He felt totally exhausted. His entire body a mass of pain. Blood was dripping from the cuts and slashes. Out the corner of his eye he could see Silverbuck's equally bloody body sprawled in the sand.

'Okay, you son of a bitch, let's just see who gets up and walks away first.'

The way he was feeling he wasn't about to take bets on who that would be.

22

A couple of Papago trackers found Bodie later that day. They had been scouting the desert area looking for one of the remaining escapees from Yuma and came across Bodie leading his weary horse and the one carrying the bodies of Cagle and Benedict.

They never found the escaped prisoner, but they knew Bodie and decided he was worth the effort of saving. They tended his wounds and did what they could before they rode him back across the desert to Yuma.

It took the town doctor a half a day to deal with the wounds, and a couple of weeks' rest, before Bodie was able to get up and about. He made no protest. He was, he admitted, bone weary and in no fit state to do anything. By the time he was able to get about and find out what was happening it was all over.

Cagle and Benedict had been buried, and despite there being a fuss about the fact the stolen gold Cagle had hidden was not going to be recovered, Bodie picked up the bounty money that had been on offer. The first thing he did was seek out the two Indians who had found him and brought him out of the desert and pay them a portion of the reward. If they hadn't shown up to help he would likely have ended up dead himself. He later found out there was a bounty on Walt Elkins and his partners. That suited Bodie. He had never been shy about collecting unexpected bounties.

He stayed around Yuma for a couple of weeks, letting his body regain its strength. He was undecided where to go until the town marshal caught up with him one day and showed him a sheath of wanted flyers that had come in with the mail.

'Figured there might be something to interest you,' he said.

Bodie thumbed through the wanted

posters, picking out a few that showed promise. There were a couple from up north. The high country where the forests were green and cool and there wasn't a desert in sight.

He had outfitted himself earlier. Bought himself a fresh horse and decided the long ride would be good for his health. He selected the flyers he wanted and headed for his hotel to check out. When he rode out of Yuma a few hours later he didn't even look back . . .